Edited by Trevor Weston

Designed by Brigitte Willgoss

ISBN 0 86112 4561
© BRIMAX BOOKS LTD 1988. All rights reserved.
Published by Brimax Books, Newmarket, England, 1988.
Second printing 1989.
Printed in Portugal by Edições ASA—Divisão Gráfica

Tales from the
ARABIAN NIGHTS

Adapted by Peter Oliver

Illustrated by Tessa Hamilton

Brimax · Newmarket · England

Tales from the Arabian Nights

Aladdin, Ali Baba and Sinbad the Sailor belong to one of the great story-telling traditions of all time: the enchanted world of the *Arabian Nights*. Their stories have delighted readers and listeners for more than a thousand years.

First translated into English a hundred years ago by the great Victorian traveller, Sir Richard Burton, the *Arabian Nights* is a strange and wonderful journey through the mysterious East. Its starting point is in the palace of the cruel King Shabriar where a beautiful Princess called Sheherezade must captivate her listener with her gift for story-telling. Her life depends on her success.

Sheherezade's stories tell of lands peopled by monstrous genies, heroes and heroines, cruel demons and fabulously wealthy kings and princes. It is a world where men and spirits meet, where massive birds carry people off, where strange islands turn into giant fish, where magic horses can fly; a world, in fact, where almost anything can happen.

This new adaptation has been specially written to allow younger readers to enjoy these marvellous tales, which include all the classics such as *Aladdin and the Wonderful Lamp, Ali Baba and the Forty Thieves*, the *Voyages of Sinbad* and the *Fisherman and the Genie*. There are also some less familiar but equally fascinating stories like *King Yunan and the Wise Man, The Ox and the Ass, The Prince Who Married a Tortoise* and *Hassan the Ropemaker*.

Handed down from generation to generation, the *Arabian Nights* has stood the tests of both place and time. It has captured people's imaginations the world over and retained its freshness and vitality to this day. This edition with its highly readable text and beautiful illustrations reflects the richness, colour and excitement that make the *Arabian Nights* one of the classics of literature.

Contents

The Arabian Nights

Many hundreds of years ago in the mysterious land of Arabia, there lived a powerful King called Shabriar. Sadly, he fell in love with an evil Princess. They married but she cheated and deceived him.

When King Shabriar discovered the Princess was plotting to kill him, he had her put to death. But the unhappy King's revenge went further. He vowed to marry a new bride every night, slaying each one in the morning.

Many beautiful Princesses married the King and lived only one night. But one evening the lovely Princess Sheherezade became his bride.

She was a great storyteller and she decided to try and save herself from the fate of the others by enchanting King Shabriar with wonderful tales of adventure, romance and bravery.

Did she live or did she die in the morning like the other Princesses? That is part of the mystery of the Arabian Nights, a story which begins when Princess Sheherezade told the King about the adventure of Ali Baba and the Forty Thieves . . .

Ali Baba and the Forty Thieves
1 Ali Baba and the Secret Cave

Ali Baba and Cassim were brothers who lived in the ancient land of Persia. Ali Baba grew up a kind and generous man. Cassim became the greediest rogue in town.

He married a rich wife and opened a shop in the bazaar. There he sold precious silks and soon became a very wealthy merchant. Cassim seldom bothered to talk to his brother.

Ali Baba married too. He lived with his wife and son in a tumbledown house on the edge of town. He worked as a humble woodman, venturing deep into the forest every morning, never returning until the sun had set.

One day in the wood, Ali Baba was busy loading logs onto his three thin donkeys when something caught his eye on the horizon. A huge cloud of dust was racing down the slope towards him. It quite startled him. But he was more frightened when out of it galloped a band of horsemen.

"Allah! Save me!" cried Ali Baba. "A gang of murderous robbers. They will kill me for what little I have."

Quickly he hid his donkeys behind some thick bushes and clambered up the nearest tree as fast as a monkey. Hiding in the branches, he watched as the horsemen stopped within a few yards of his tree. He held his breath, his hands trembling like leaves in a breeze, and counted the men.

There were forty of them, ferocious and fat, each one carrying bulging sacks; booty from their last expedition, no doubt, thought Ali Baba.

The Captain of the men leapt from his panting horse. Ali Baba was horrified to see him walk towards the tree he was clinging to. 'I am discovered,' he thought.

Ali Baba would have leapt for his life at that moment, but just then the Captain turned away and walked up to a huge wall of rock beside the tree. He stopped, looked around and then faced the rock again.

'What is he doing?' wondered Ali Baba, peeping through the leaves. 'This is all very strange.'

The Captain took one more look around him to make sure nobody was watching and then, much to Ali Baba's surprise, began talking to the rock, his hand high in the air.

"O mighty door, do as I bid, and obey the magic words," he cried. "Open Sesame!"

Ali Baba was astounded to see what happened next. Instantly a huge door appeared in the rock and suddenly began to open.

"By the Great God, Allah, this is magic," whispered Ali Baba under his breath.

Once the door was open, the Captain and his men trooped in with their sacks. The mysterious door closed behind them with a stony thud.

Ali Baba hardly dared move for a while. He thought about escaping back to town, but it was not long before the massive door opened again and the men came out.

The Captain raised his hand and bid the door close. "Close Sesame!" The door obeyed his command as it had before. It swung shut and vanished. The rock was just a rock again. Ali Baba could not even see where the door had been.

The robbers jumped onto their horses and rode off. Soon they were just another cloud in the distance. Ali Baba waited until they were over the hill and then clambered down from his tree. He was about to run off home with his donkeys when he took one last glance at the rock.

'I wonder . . . I wonder,' thought Ali Baba. 'I wonder if the magic words will work for me?'

Nervously, Ali Baba approached the rock. "Open . . ." Ali Baba hardly dare say the words. "Open Sesame!"

At last the words were out and Ali Baba stepped back in fright as the door obeyed his command. It appeared and opened. Poor Ali Baba, he was so frightened he didn't know what to do. He walked towards the door. He walked away again. His legs didn't want to carry him through.

At last he plucked up enough courage. Ali Baba edged his way through the doorway. What he saw took his breath away.

He had expected to find a dark cavern. But instead his eyes lit up at the wonderful sight of huge heaps of gold and silver and sacks of sparkling diamonds and pearls. The cavern, lit by a single beam of light coming from a chink in the roof, shone with every treasure under the sun.

"A treasure house of the gods!" murmured Ali Baba in astonishment, hardly noticing the cavern door closing behind him. "These robbers have collected a fortune big enough to ransom all the kings in Arabia."

Slowly Ali Baba regained his wits. 'My family is so poor,' he thought.

'Surely the robbers wouldn't notice if I took just a few trinkets, a few gold coins to help feed and clothe my wife and son.'

Ali Baba found a small bag and filled it with coins. The job was quickly done and, after saying the magic words to open and close the door, he was on his way home again.

His wife was amazed when she saw what he had found. "But Ali Baba," she said, "you are not a thief."

"I haven't stolen them," said Ali Baba. "We are poor and the coins are a gift from kindly gods."

Ali Baba's wife accepted his explanation but she wanted to find out how much gold was in the bag. "I will go to Cassim's wife and borrow her scales to weigh all the gold coins," she said.

Cassim's wife was very surprised when Ali Baba's wife asked for the scales. She was so suspicious that she smeared the bottom of them with sticky grease. Her little trick worked too. When Ali Baba's wife returned the scales that night, stuck to the bottom was one cold coin.

"Ho! Now where did Ali Baba get that from?" cried Cassim's wife. She ran to tell Cassim what had happened.

"Curses on my brother," said the jealous Cassim. "How did he come by such gold?" Cassim hated the idea of his brother having so much money. He was so envious he hardly slept a wink that night. Before dawn he ran to Ali Baba's house.

"Scoundrel brother," he panted. "Tell me where you found this gold or I shall have you thrown in the deepest dungeon I can find." Ali Baba realised his secret was discovered. He confessed the whole story to Cassim, not forgetting to mention the magic words.

Cassim rushed out of the door, ran home, collected his ten donkeys and rode off to the rock.

"Open Sesame!" he cried. The door appeared and opened as before. Like Ali Baba, his eyes shone at the fantastic sight inside. He didn't notice the door slam shut behind him because he was already too busy filling sacks with priceless gems and gold coins.

He filled as many sacks as his

donkeys could carry and stacked them by the door. "Now, I'll just open the door again," Cassim told himself. His mouth opened . . . but no words came out. Cassim was so excited at what he had seen in the cave that the magic words had slipped right out of his head.

"Open Celery . . . Open Cabbage . . . Open Carrots." He tried so hard to remember the words. But it was no use. He had forgotten them and the door stayed firmly shut. Cassim was locked inside. He shivered and shook. The sparkling jewels glinted at him like demons. They couldn't warm his heart any more. The chill of the night froze his greedy thoughts forever.

Princess Sheherezade stopped speaking. She could see that the King was spellbound.

"What happens next?" asked the King excitedly.

"It is late, o master," said the Princess. "Shall I continue tomorrow night?"

"I must know what happens to Cassim and Ali Baba. It would be a thousand tortures not to hear more."

And so it was, the next night, that the Princess revealed the rest of Ali Baba's story . . .

2 The Fate of Cassim and the Robbers

Cassim was trapped in the cave. All night he tried to remember the magic words without success. In the morning the sound of horses' hooves outside the cavern sent fresh shudders of fear through him. A moment later he heard the words he had so desperately tried to remember. "Open Sesame!" It was the Captain's voice.

Now it was too late. The robbers had returned to their den with more stolen goods. Cassim hid behind a huge sack of gold. But the Captain had already seen the donkeys outside. Once inside the cavern, he soon discovered the trembling figure of Cassim.

"Oh, villainous thief. You would steal from thieves, would you?" he cried. "Prepare to die!" The Captain drew out his gleaming sword and advanced on Cassim. With one thrust he was dead.

When Cassim did not return that night, his wife became very

worried. She went to Ali Baba. He guessed immediately what had happened and rode off to the rock the next morning.

Seeing that the robbers were not about, he opened the door. Cassim's body lay across the very sacks he had filled so greedily.

"O Cassim," said Ali Baba sadly, "I only took a few coins to help my family. You were too greedy and now it has cost you your life."

Ali Baba laid Cassim on his donkey and returned home with the news. On the way he heard the sound of the robbers galloping back to the cavern after another night of robbing.

The Captain was furious when he saw Cassim's body had gone. "Someone else must know our secret," he growled. "We must go to town and find out who. The man I killed must have a brother or another relative. We will seek him out and kill him."

The Captain and the robbers, fearing capture, dared not go into town without disguising themselves. "I shall dress up as an oil merchant," decided the Captain, "and I will hide all my men in oil jars."

That is how the forty thieves reached town, hidden in forty large oil jars carried on twenty donkeys. It didn't take the Captain long to discover whose brother had died recently and soon the donkeys and their devilish cargo drew up outside Ali Baba's house.

The Captain knocked at the door. Ali Baba's faithful and beautiful servant Morgiana answered the knock. "Kind lady, I have just arrived in town," explained the Captain, "and I need somewhere to sleep for the night."

Morgiana found Ali Baba. He was happy to welcome the stranger to his house, not recognising the disguised man as the Captain of the robbers. "Put your donkeys in the stable," said Ali Baba, "and then I will prepare a feast for you."

It was a splendid feast and afterwards the Captain made an excuse, saying he was going to the stable to make sure his donkeys were all right. Instead he crept between the jars, whispering to each man, "I will return at midnight. When you hear my voice, take hold of your daggers and come out. Then we shall kill Ali Baba."

Soon everyone was in bed . . . everyone, that is, except Morgiana who was still working in the kitchen. She worked so late that the oil in her lamp ran out.

"No matter," she said, "I can borrow some oil from one of the merchant's jars." Taking an oil pot, Morgiana went to the stable. The donkeys were snoring and the row of oil jars stood silent.

Now, jars don't talk. Morgiana knew that. Yet one of them spoke to her. "Is it time to come out yet?" said a voice.

Morgiana froze on the spot. "A jar that speaks?" she whispered to herself. "By Allah, it is not the jar, but someone hiding inside." The girl was frightened, but she kept her wits. She realised someone was plotting against her master. In the deepest voice she could muster, she replied: "No, it is not time yet."

She was very surprised when voices from all the other jars replied: "We shall wait for your signal."

Morgiana rushed back into her kitchen, wondering what she should do. An idea quickly came to her. Filling a huge cauldron with fat, she put it on her flaming stove. Bubble! Sizzle! The fat began to melt and boil.

Tiptoeing back into the stable with the cauldron, Morgiana quietly placed it in one corner. She took a great ladle and filled it with the scalding fat. The thieves, crouching in the jars, were unaware of the dreadful fate about to befall them.

Morgiana took the ladle and, lifting the lid of the nearest oil jar, poured in the burning liquid. She did the same at every jar. In a few

minutes all the thieves were dead.

She returned to the kitchen to wait. She sat down in a chair by the door, leaving it a little ajar to see into the corridor outside. When the night was at its blackest, she saw the oil merchant creep past and sneak into the stable. "It is time!" he hissed.

There wasn't a sound. The Captain was puzzled but when he discovered all his men were dead, he was horrified.

"I underestimated you, Ali Baba," he cried. "A thousand curses on your head." Fearing for his own life, the Captain galloped out of the stable, leapt over a wall and fled into the night.

Morgiana told Ali Baba the whole astounding story in the morning. He was very grateful to her for having saved his life. "Loyal servant, I will not forget your brave deeds," he said.

Meanwhile the Captain had escaped back to the forest and was busy planning revenge. "I must kill Ali Baba or he will steal all my treasures."

The Captain's plan was very clever. He would disguise himself as a shopkeeper and seek out Ali Baba's son. He wanted to become friends with him and find favour in the eyes of Ali Baba.

His devilish scheme worked. As the days passed, the Captain and Ali Baba's son became close friends. Ali Baba fell into the trap and decided to reward the false shopkeeper for the kindness to his son. "Noble sir, you must come to my house and feast with me."

The Captain was delighted to accept. 'Now, Ali Baba,' he thought, 'I have you at my mercy. You will not escape me this time.'

The night of the feast arrived and the sly Captain sat down with Ali Baba and his son. Ali Baba's son stared dreamily at Morgiana. He had long been in love with the pretty servant girl. But Morgiana's sharp eyes were occupied with other things – Ali Baba's guest.

'It is the Captain of the robbers,' she realised with a fright.

Morgiana served the food and hurried back to the kitchen. Time was running out. The Captain was eagerly fingering the dagger in his belt. His hand tightened around the handle when Morgiana swept back into the room with a young slave boy. He was carrying a tambourine.

"Lord and master, let me dance for you and your guest," said Morgiana, hurriedly.

Ali Baba was very pleased with the idea. "Yes, Morgiana, come dance for us."

The Captain scowled as the boy struck up a lively beat on his instrument and Morgiana began to dance. She danced so beautifully that the Captain was enchanted. He forgot about his deadly plan for the moment.

Morgiana's coloured robes swirled about her as the dance grew livelier. Faster and faster she moved, until the Captain was entranced. He never saw the dagger which she suddenly produced from her belt. One moment it was in her hand, flashing in the air, the next it was buried in the Captain's heart.

"Morgiana! What have you done?" cried Ali Baba. He could not believe his eyes as his guest fell stone-dead on the floor.

Morgiana knelt at Ali Baba's feet. "My lord, I did this for you. Look under the man's robes. You will find a dagger which was intended for your heart. Look under his disguise and you will see that he is not an honest shopkeeper. He is the Captain of the thieves."

Ali Baba looked at the man in astonishment. All Morgiana had said was true. "Twice you have saved my life," he said. "Twice I will reward you. You will be a servant no more. First you will marry my son and second I will give you all the precious gifts in the world."

Ali Baba was true to his word. He made them both very rich since, with the Captain and the robbers all dead, only Ali Baba knew the secret of the cave and the magic words.

Ali Baba lived to a great age but before he died he told his son the secret of the robber's storehouse. That secret has been passed down from father to son for hundreds of years. Somewhere that cave still exists and such was the treasure stored inside, that it will keep Ali Baba's descendants rich forever.

When Princess Sheherezade finished the story of Ali Baba, she knelt at King Shabriar's feet and asked if he had enjoyed the tale.

"Yes, very much," replied the King. "I have never heard such a good story."

Princess Sheherezade looked at the King and said, "If you will allow me to live, I shall tell you an even better story tomorrow night."

The King was delighted. "You shall live another day if you tell me the story."

So, the next night, Princess Sheherezade began the story of the Fisherman and the Genie . . .

The Fisherman and the Genie
1 The Brass Bottle

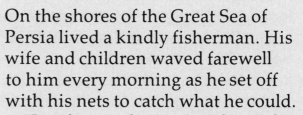

On the shores of the Great Sea of Persia lived a kindly fisherman. His wife and children waved farewell to him every morning as he set off with his nets to catch what he could.

"Let the seas bring us riches," they all used to say.

The fisherman would smile and reply, "If the gods of the sea send a few fishes my way, we should all be grateful."

One morning he waded into the sea and cast his net. When the time came to haul it in, the fisherman was surprised to find it was almost too heavy to pull to shore. He heaved and he hauled. "I must have caught the biggest fish in the sea," he said aloud.

The fisherman struggled to heave his nets ashore. At last the sea gave up its mysterious prize. Out of the net tumbled, not a monster fish, but a huge brass jar. It stood almost as high as the fisherman, who quickly spotted that its lid was firmly held on by an ancient lead seal.

"Now, this is something," puffed the fisherman, out of breath. "It looks valuable enough to sell at the bazaar. It must be worth a piece of gold." He took a knife from his belt and freed the lead seal. The lid snapped open and he looked inside.

"How very odd!" he puzzled. "The jar is empty and yet it is so heavy."

Psssshhh! Fizz! Zoom! A column of smoke burst out of the jar and shot towards the heavens. The fisherman jumped backwards in fright, tripped on a stone and fell on his back.

21

High in the sky he saw the column of smoke twist violently and turn into the figure of a giant Genie. His head touched the clouds and his legs, as long as two tree trunks, planted themselves with two great thuds beside him on the ground. The Genie's eyes shone fiercely and his teeth looked like huge rocks in a monstrous cave.

The fisherman was terrified. He had heard stories about Genies before. He knew they were spirits with tremendous powers. He also knew that they could be good or evil. Which one was this Genie?

"Who are you?" asked the fisherman, his teeth chattering with fright. "What do you want?"

The Genie's answer made his legs shake: "O, unlucky fisherman. You will die a terrible death within the hour," said the booming voice.

"Why do you want to kill me?" said the fisherman, at last getting to his feet. "I have done nothing wrong."

But the Genie would not listen. "Just tell me how you want to die and I will kill you."

The fisherman could not see how he could save himself. But perhaps he could win himself a little time to think. "Why do you want to kill me?" he said. "Tell me your story first." The Genie hesitated for a moment and then decided to explain to the fisherman where he had come from.

"I was a very bad Genie once," he began. "I was so bad that the spirit gods locked me in this jar and threw it out to sea. There I have been trapped for a thousand years, rolling around on the seabed."

"A thousand years?" said the astonished fisherman.

"Yes! A thousand years," thundered the Genie. "When I had been there a hundred years I promised myself that if anyone freed me I would make them richer than they ever dreamed possible."

"*I* have freed you," said the fisherman.

The Genie frowned. "But no one found me after a hundred years," he continued. "Nine hundred more years passed and I swore that I would kill the first man to find me. You are that man. So prepare to die."

"Spare my life," cried the fisherman. "I am a poor man with a wife and children."

The Genie was becoming angry. "There is nothing you can say to change my mind."

Now the fisherman may have been poor but he was also quite cunning. "Before you kill me," he said, "I must say one thing. I cannot believe that someone as large as you ever fitted into that small jar."

"What!" stormed the Genie. "You do not believe I lived in that jar for a thousand years." The fisherman said he did not and, what is more, would only believe it if he saw it with his own eyes.

By now the Genie was very angry. "I'll show you!" he roared. The huge figure twisted, squirmed, wriggled . . . and vanished into a column of smoke again. With the sound of howling wind, it shot back into the jar.

Hardly had the last puff of smoke vanished inside, than the fisherman grabbed the lid of the jar and snapped it back on top. The Genie was trapped. "Now!" said the fisherman, triumphantly. "How would you like to die? By Allah, I shall throw you back into the sea, you monster of the deep."

There was a ghostly howl from the jar as the Genie realised he had been tricked back into his prison. "No! No! No! Let me out," he screeched.

The fisherman was not going to risk letting the demon out again. "I shall throw you back in the sea," he said. "Then I shall build a house at this very place and if anyone comes here to fish I shall warn them not to. You will stay in your jar at the bottom of the sea forever."

The Genie pleaded: "Come, let me out. I was only playing a joke on you. I wasn't really going to kill you."

"You're lying," said the fisherman, dragging the jar towards the water. "Nothing you can say will stop me now. You will lie buried in the sea for another thousand years."

The Genie begged for his freedom. "Forgive me. Please open the jar," he said. "If you let me out, I promise to make you rich."

The fisherman put down the jar for a moment. He was not a cruel man. He was really very kind and he didn't want to throw the Genie back into the sea. "If I free you, will you promise not to hurt me?" he asked.

"You have my word," came the answer from the jar. "If you free me I will make you richer than you ever dreamed possible."

The fisherman was still very frightened about what the Genie might do. But he decided to trust him. Slowly, very slowly, the fisherman undid the lid of the jar again.

Psssshhh! Fizz! Zoom! Once more the column of smoke burst out and flew into the sky. The huge Genie appeared as horrible as before, his burning eyes as bright as two suns. With one flick of his gigantic toes, the Genie sent the jar flying far out to sea. There it sank to be lost forever.

The fisherman trembled. 'I have been foolish,' he thought. 'He is still going to kill me.'

The Genie could see how terrified the fisherman was and began to bellow with laughter. The sound echoed through the heavens. "Don't you believe a Genie can keep his word?" said the towering figure. "You should have more faith. I will do everything I said."

Then, beckoning the fisherman to follow him, he walked off towards some distant mountains. The fisherman did as he was asked and ran after him, making sure he was not trampled under the giant's feet.

They travelled together for a long way, a long walk for the fisherman in any case. The Genie seemed to cover a mile with every step. Finally they reached a mountain lake, nestling beneath four hills. It was a ghostly place.

The Genie stepped into the lake, again asking his companion to follow. The water hardly came to the Genie's ankles, but the fisherman was soon up to his waist.

It was then that the fisherman saw an astonishing sight. Swimming all around him were strange fish of different colours; some white, some blue, others red or yellow. They had the saddest eyes he had ever seen. No fish ever looked unhappier.

"Cast your net here," said the Genie. "Catch one fish of each colour and then take them to the Sultan in the city. If you do that, you will become a rich man."

The fisherman did as he was told and as the last fish wriggled into his net, the Genie spoke again: "Now, I must go. I have not seen the world for a thousand years and I have so much to see and do. Farewell."

The fisherman would have liked to say goodbye too but the Genie struck the ground with his foot and the earth instantly swallowed him up in a puff of smoke.

When the fisherman recovered from his surprise, he thought for a moment, remembering the Genie's words. He waded ashore, put the fish in his bag and set off for the city to find the Sultan.

'What a strange day,' thought the fisherman. 'But if the Genie is speaking the truth, I shall be rich.'

The sun was just beginning to set when he saw the city in the distance . . .

Princess Sheherezade broke off from telling her story. King Shabriar was most disappointed.

"It is such a good story, but what happens next?" he asked.

"If you will let me live another day, I shall tell you about the magic fish tomorrow night," replied the Princess.

"I must hear the end of the story," he said. "You must go on."

So the next night came and Princess Sheherezade continued the adventures of the fisherman . . .

2 The Magic Fish

The fisherman reached the Sultan's palace and was met at the gates by two guards. "I have a present for the Sultan," said the fisherman.

A message was sent to the mighty Sultan who was sitting with his courtiers eagerly awaiting dinner. "Send the fisherman in," he ordered. "I hope he has brought me something special to eat."

When the Sultan saw the fish, he was quite bewildered. "I have never seen such fish," he said. "White, blue, red and yellow. Give them to the cook. I shall eat them tonight."

The fisherman was handsomely rewarded. The Sultan gave him a hundred pieces of gold. He hurried home to tell his wife and children the good news. 'All this good luck,' he thought. 'I must be dreaming.'

Meanwhile, at the Sultan's palace, strange things were happening. Just as the cook put the fish into the frying pan, the kitchen wall opened up and out stepped a beautiful Princess. Beautiful she was, but certainly not kind. There was an evil look on her face, and in her hands she carried a stick. She beat the fish over their heads and cried, "Fish! Fish! Is the fat hot enough for you?"

The cook fainted when she saw the fish stand up on their tails in the pan and reply, "Save us! Save us!"

The cook woke up soon after and saw the blackened fish. "What will the Sultan say?" she gasped, thinking he would be very angry with her. She went to tell the Sultan all that had happened.

The Sultan did not believe her and immediately called for the fisherman to be found. He arrived the next morning and bowed to the powerful man. He was sure he was going to be punished.

"There is some magic about these fish," said the Sultan. "You must go and catch me four more fish; one white, one blue, one red and one yellow. Bring them to me for dinner tonight."

The fisherman returned to the strange lake and did as the Sultan asked. He hurried back to the palace with the fish. The Sultan thanked the fisherman and gave him another hundred pieces of gold. He went home even happier than before.

In the palace kitchen that night, the Sultan hid behind a pillar and watched as the cook placed the fish in the frying pan. No sooner had the fat begun to sizzle than the kitchen wall burst apart again. Out leapt a huge and ugly slave, his cruel eyes searching for the fish. He too had a stick. He saw the fish in the pan and smacked them on their heads. "Fry, fish! Fry!"

They also stood up on their tails in the pan and cried, "Save us! Save us!" The slave scowled and stirred up the fat with his stick. The fish turned to cinders once more and the slave vanished through the wall.

"Demons and devils!" said the

Sultan. "There must be a strange story behind these fish. Who are the Princess and the slave who came through the wall? How did the fish speak? What a puzzle."

The fisherman was called to the palace again and the Sultan asked him where the fish had been caught. The fisherman explained that he had caught them in the mountain lake which lay between four black hills.

"I know every inch of my kingdom," said the Sultan, "but I have never ever seen, or heard of that lake, or those hills. How far away are they?"

"No more than half an hour's walk," answered the fisherman.

"You must take me there," said the Sultan.

That night the fisherman led the Sultan, his courtiers and slaves, out of the palace gates and deep into the darkness beyond.

It was late when they reached the lake. The moon lit up the four black hills and glistened on the water below. The Sultan could not believe his eyes. He asked his courtiers if any of them had ever seen the lake or the hills before. None of them had.

'This is a very strange mystery,' thought the Sultan. 'I will not return to my palace until I have solved the riddle of the lake and the fish.' He lay in his tent that night wondering what to do. At last he decided that he must go alone into the black hills to find the answer. Before the sun rose the next morning, the Sultan put on his sword and slipped away from the camp by the lake.

His courtiers were puzzled when they awoke to find the Sultan gone. They decided to wait by the lake until he returned.

The Sultan travelled for a day and a night through the mountains, looking everywhere for clues to the mystery. As dawn broke the next day, he saw something gleaming darkly in the distance. He kept on walking until he found himself in front of the massive gates of a palace. It was built of huge black stones. The gates were open but no one was to be seen. 'The palace must be empty,' he decided.

"Hello!" he shouted. "Is there anyone here?"

Silence. Not a sound. The Sultan walked through the gates and found himself in a courtyard. Still no sound, nor sign of any living thing. He saw a door in one corner and tiptoed through it. Inside was a great hall. Colourful silks and gold decorations hung from the walls. 'Whoever lived here must have been very rich,' thought the Sultan, moving towards a door which led out of the hall.

He came into another courtyard. In the middle of it was a towering fountain, guarded by four statues of golden lions. Water sparkled out of the fountain like glistening pearls and diamonds. The Sultan stared at the scene. He could not understand why there were no people. He drank from the fountain and then sat down to rest.

Just then he heard a faint sound. He listened closely and realised that it was someone crying. The sobs came from behind a curtained door which led off from the courtyard. The Sultan got up and walked across. Pulling the curtain aside, he entered a small room. There, sitting on a gold embroidered cushion, was a young man.

He wore a crown on his head but

his face was lined with tears. The sad young man was undoubtedly of royal blood. His eyes looked up in surprise at seeing the strange visitor.

The Sultan introduced himself and explained his arrival at the palace. "I have come to discover the truth behind the mountain lake and the coloured fish . . . but first I must find out why you are alone and so sad." The young man pulled aside the cloak he was wearing. The Sultan was startled to see that his legs were made of stone.

"Poor man," said the Sultan. "How did this happen?"

The young man looked at the Sultan and saw that he was a kindly person. "If I tell you my story," he said, "you will also discover the secret of the fish."

"Then please tell me," said the Sultan.

The young man settled himself on his cushion and began his story. "I am the King of the Black Isles . . ."

"Who is this King of the Black Isles?" said King Shabriar. "Why is he so sad?"

"If you let me live, I will tell you the rest of the story tomorrow," answered Sheherezade.

The King agreed once more and so, on the next night, Princess Sheherezade revealed the secret of the fish . . .

3 The King of the Black Isles

"I am the King of the Black Isles," the young man told the Sultan, "but my kingdom and its people were stolen from me by an ogress and her evil slave."

"What ogress? What slave?" interrupted the Sultan, thinking about the Princess and the slave who had appeared in his kitchen and beaten the fish in the frying pan.

"The ogress was my wife," said the King of the Black Isles. "The slave was the evil man she ran off with."

"Tell me more," said the Sultan.

The King explained that he had loved his wife dearly. Then one day he had overheard her and the slave plotting to destroy his city and imprison his people.

"I pulled out my sword," said the King, "and ran the slave through. I thought I had killed him but I discovered later that I had only slashed his neck. Such was the wound that he lost the power of speech. He could not talk any more."

"What happened to your wife, the ogress?" asked the Sultan.

"I wanted to kill her too but before I could move again, she cast a wicked spell. Suddenly I was half stone and half man as you see me now."

"O, poor King. What happened next?" asked the Sultan.

"She used her powers to bewitch my city. She turned my kingdom of four islands into four black hills and then magically turned all my people into fish of many colours; white, blue, red and yellow. The city itself, she changed into a lake."

"Where are the ogress and the slave now?" asked the Sultan, his eyes burning for revenge.

"Each day my wife comes in and feeds me pieces of boiled rat and bones. Then she beats me. The slave still lies in a room on the other side of the courtyard," said the King. "He is recovering from my sword wound, but he still cannot speak."

The Sultan left the room and silently crossed the courtyard. He opened the door and saw the slave asleep on some rugs on the floor. The slave awoke just as the Sultan was drawing his sword.

He tried to cry out but he had no voice. The Sultan killed him with a thrust to the heart. The Sultan hid the body, carefully removing the slave's cloak. He put it on and, disguised as the slave, lay down on the slave's bed. Beneath the rugs he hid his sword.

In the morning, the ogress arrived to see how her slave was. The room was dimly lit and she could not see that another man had taken the slave's place. She knelt down beside the bed and spoke. "I wish I had powers to bring back your voice. I can only pray that one day you will speak to me again."

At that moment the Sultan whispered in the weakest voice he could manage, "Let me have some wine."

"Allah be praised," cried the ogress. "You spoke. You are cured."

"Yes," said the Sultan, disguising his voice, "and my voice will be completely cured if you free your husband from your spell. He cries all night and I cannot sleep."

"I will do anything you want," she said.

The ogress filled a bowl with water and took it into the room where the King of the Black Isles lay sleeping.

32

"O god of devils, devils of spirits," she screamed, as the water began to bubble and boil. "Spirits of evil, take away my spell!"

The King awoke with a start and saw that his legs were flesh again. The ogress looked at him with a cursed eye. "I have cured you. Now leave this palace and never return. If you do, by my friends, the devils and spirits, I will kill you."

She quickly returned to the slave's room, where the disguised Sultan still lay. "Have you done it?" he asked.

"He is free again," she replied.

"Then," said the Sultan, "there is just one more thing you can do for me. The people you turned into fish cry out every night. Set them free as well."

No sooner had he said the words than the unsuspecting ogress ran off to the lake. There she undid her horrible curse.

The fish raised their heads and stood up. In an instant they became men, women and children again. The hills turned back into islands and the lake vanished. In its place, the city appeared. Its streets were full of people and the bazaar was bustling with merchants doing their business.

The Sultan's courtiers and slaves, who had been camping at the lake waiting for their master to return, were astonished. Suddenly they found themselves sitting in the middle of the bazaar.

The ogress returned to the palace and went to the slave's room. "I have done all you asked," she said proudly. "All the people are free again and the lake has become a city once more."

The Sultan pretended to be grateful. "Come close to me. My voice is still weak. But I can feel it getting stronger all the time."

The ogress reached the side of his bed. It was only then that she saw it was not the slave who spoke. But it was too late. The Sultan's hand was on his sword and a moment later the ogress was dead.

The Sultan rose from his bed and went in search of the King of the Black Isles. They met at the palace gates. "Your kingdom is restored," he said. "Your people are alive and your city is returned."

The King was so happy he could not thank the Sultan enough. "How can I return your kind deeds?"

"You must come with me to my city," said the Sultan. "We will celebrate with a huge feast."

The King smiled. "How far away do you think your city lies?" he asked.

"It is only a short journey," said the Sultan. "One day's travel at the most."

Immediately the King of the Black Isles laughed out aloud. "I am afraid you have been bewitched by the magic of the ogress too," he said. "I know your city. It is a year's journey from here. Her magic made it seem shorter."

The Sultan understood it all at last. "So that's why I had never heard of the lake and the hills. But no matter, my friend. The magic is now gone and even if it takes a year, you must still come to my city."

So they left the palace and began their journey. Soon they reached the city of the Black Isles and found the Sultan's courtiers and slaves. They were as surprised at the Sultan's story as he was at their tale of suddenly finding themselves in the bazaar.

It was indeed another year before they finally reached the Sultan's palace. The whole city came out to welcome him. The people had almost given up hope of ever seeing their Sultan again.

There were many celebrations. The Sultan sat the King at his right hand and dressed him in the richest robes and swore friendship for ever. There was one other friend he did not forget: the fisherman.

35

"Bring the fisherman to my palace," ordered the Sultan.

The fisherman was sure the Sultan wanted to punish him for giving him the strange fish. But nothing could be further from the Sultan's mind.

"You are the good man who led to the discovery of the King of the Black Isles," said the Sultan. "You alone showed me the way. You shall be handsomely rewarded. Do you have any sons or daughters?"

"Yes," said the puzzled fisherman. "I have two daughters and a son, all unmarried."

"Bring them to my palace," he cried.

Their arrival brought a happy end to the story of the fisherman and the Genie. One daughter married the Sultan's son and the other became the wife of the King of the Black Isles. The fisherman's son became the Sultan's Chief Treasurer.

The fisherman himself became one of the richest men of all. The Sultan gave him untold riches and loved him like a brother.

He did not go fishing again but he never forgot the Genie who promised to make him richer than he ever dreamed possible.

King Shabriar had been truly enchanted by the story of the fisherman. "I wonder where that mischievous Genie is now?" he said.

"No one ever saw him again," said Princess Sheherezade. "I doubt that even Duban, the wisest man in the East, could tell you."

"Duban?" said the King. "Who is Duban?"

"O, master, if you let me live another night, I will tell you all about him."

"Let me hear about this great wise man," said the King.

And so, the next night, Princess Sheherezade began the story of King Yunan and Duban the Wise Man . . .

King Yunan and the Wise Man

King Yunan was a rich and powerful man. There was nothing in the world he could not afford to buy. His fingers glittered with gold and silver rings and his clothes were made of the rarest silk. Hundreds of courtiers and slaves obeyed his every wish.

Yet one thing troubled him greatly. He suffered from an illness which nobody could cure. His face was covered in boils. The King drank potions and swallowed powders every day, but not even the cleverest men in his kingdom could heal him.

Now one day, Duban, an ancient wise man and a mighty healer, arrived in the city. What a sight he was! He rode upon a huge bony camel and his saddle-bags bulged with books, bottles and boxes. The King soon heard about Duban and called him to the palace.

"They tell me you are the greatest healer of them all," said the King. "Can you cure me?"

"Great and powerful King," said Duban, "I have the power to make potions which will quickly rid you of your sickness."

The King was overjoyed to hear the wise man's words and it was arranged that Duban would return the next day. That night Duban went to his lodgings and studied his dusty books. Before dawn he went out into the fields to gather magic herbs and secret ingredients. By the time the sun was high in the sky, the potion was ready.

The King eagerly awaited Duban's arrival. So did all his courtiers, emirs, chamberlains, grandees, lords and, not least, the Vizier, the King's chief adviser.

"This is the potion," said Duban. "Just rub the mixture into the palms of your hands and your illness will have gone by morning."

The King did as he was told. He could hardly sleep that night, but when he rose from his golden bed the next morning the wise man's potion had done its work. "I'm cured," exclaimed the King.

No one had seen the King so happy. All day he laughed and smiled, showered favours on his courtiers and gave money to all the beggars in his city. As evening fell, he called Duban to his court.

"Duban, you are indeed a great healer," said the King. "You will be handsomely rewarded."

The King gave Duban many bags of gold, dressed him in the richest robes and made him a powerful man in his court. "Ask of me anything," said the grateful King, "and you shall have it."

Duban wanted nothing. "My reward is to cure you," he said. "There is nothing more precious you can give me." But the King's gratitude

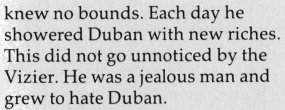

knew no bounds. Each day he showered Duban with new riches. This did not go unnoticed by the Vizier. He was a jealous man and grew to hate Duban.

'This Duban is becoming more important and powerful than me,' thought the wicked Vizier. 'I must bring about his downfall.'

The scheming Vizier went to the King one day. "Beware, my Lord," he said. "There is a man in your court who is not what he seems. He is a spy from another country."

The King was worried. "Who is this man?"

"It is Duban, the wise man," snarled the Vizier.

The King could not believe it. "Fie on you, Vizier. Duban is the man who cured me. I would share my kingdom with him."

But every day the Vizier told the King more and more terrible stories. "He is undoubtedly a spy and a wicked magician," said the Vizier. "If he can cure you by rubbing a potion in your palm, he can kill you just as easily."

The King tried hard not to believe the stories. But the Vizier was a very good liar. Gradually the King became convinced that the Vizier spoke the truth. "If he is a spy," said the King, "then he must be executed. Bring Duban to me."

Duban arrived, expecting to receive more presents. He was astounded when the King pronounced: "Duban, you are a spy who wants to kill me and destroy my kingdom. It will cost you your life."

The King turned to his Vizier and ordered that the executioner be brought. Duban was speechless. But the sight of the executioner and his glinting sword loosened his tongue. "What have I done to deserve this?" he cried. "I have cured you. What sort of reward is this?"

Nothing could change the King's mind.

But the next words spoken by Duban sent a chill through him: "Spare me and Allah will spare you," he said. "Slay me and Allah will slay you. Mark my words."

"Prepare yourself to die," said the King.

Duban, seeing that his fate was sealed, made one last request. "You are a mighty and powerful King. Grant me a favour. Let me first return to my lodgings. I have many magical books there. There is one which you would dearly love to possess."

"What book is that?" puzzled the King.

"A book which holds the secrets of life and death," answered Duban. "In its pages lies your future. On page three rests your fate."

The King agreed to put off the execution until the next day. But before he left the palace, Duban made one more strange request. "You must promise not to open the book until you have cut off my head."

"Is that part of the magic?" asked the King.

"Yes," said Duban. "Once your executioner's sword has done its work, my head will talk to you."

"A talking head?" asked the King. "What will it tell me?"

"My head will answer any question you ask it," said Duban. "Now I must go. I shall return in the morning."

News of the execution spread quickly around the city. Huge crowds lined the streets the next morning and the King's court was filled with people. A magic book and a talking head . . . this was something to see.

Duban arrived as he had promised. Under his arm was a huge and ancient book. "Now," Duban told the King, "here is the book. But remember, you must not open its pages until your executioner has cut off my head."

The King said farewell to Duban and signalled to the executioner. Duban and his head were quickly parted.

The head was placed on a silver tray. The King looked at it. The Vizier looked at it. All the courtiers looked at it. Surely a head could not talk! The King began to laugh. "See! This head will not talk. Duban lied."

Just then a voice spoke. "The Vizier is the liar." The words echoed around the court. Everybody looked at the head. Aghast, they saw that it was speaking.

The King and the courtiers trembled so much the room began to shake.

"Listen to me," said the head, eerily. "Now you can open the book."

The King, an icy shiver of fear running down his spine, picked up the book. The great dusty cover opened easily enough. But then he tried to turn the first page. "It will not open," said the King. "It is stuck."

He felt another great tremble as the head spoke again. "Lick your finger with your tongue, and once moist it will turn the page."

The King obeyed. He licked his finger and managed to turn it. But the second page was stuck too. The King licked his finger again and the page fell open. The third page was firmly stuck like the others.

"Lick your finger again," said the head. "The third page will open."

The King licked his finger and once more placed it on the edge of the page. The third page was revealed at last.

"What's this?" cried the King. "There's nothing written on the third page." Indeed the third page was absolutely blank. Not a word was written there. "You have fooled me, Duban," shouted the King.

The head spoke. "You must look more closely. Your own death is written there. I said that if you spared me, Allah would spare you, and if you slayed me, Allah would slay you. You have written your death with your own finger."

41

The King was very puzzled. But then he began to feel terribly ill. His throat burned and his stomach felt as if he had swallowed a hundred red-hot coals. Soon he was in agony and fell to the ground. At last he understood what the head had said.

"You put poison on the pages," groaned the King. "I have poisoned myself with my fingers."

"Yes," answered the head. "You have brought this death on yourself. I was innocent and you killed me. Now you must face Allah's justice and share my fate." With those words, the King died and the head closed its eyes.

It never spoke again.

King Shabriar was amazed at the story. "The wise man Duban may yet teach me a lesson," he said. "He who kills an innocent person can expect no mercy."

Princess Sheherezade smiled at the King. "You must take what lessons you will from my stories," she said. "But if you listen longer, I have another tale of magic to tell."

"Your smile is beginning to enchant me," said the King. "It enchants me like your stories. Tell me your next tale."

"You must wait until tomorrow night," said the Princess.

And so, the next night, Princess Sheherezade began the story of The Magic Horse . . .

The Magic Horse

1 The Magician's Gift

Emperor Sabur was a mighty ruler of Persia. Wealthy, generous and wise, he loved the poor as much as any of his people. The Emperor was always ready to help anyone in need.

He adored his children too, a son and two daughters. He called the Princesses his 'sun' and 'moon' because they were so beautiful. "Lucky will be the husbands who marry you," he used to say.

There were many men in the city who would have given anything to marry either of them. The Emperor turned down many suitors. "You are good men," he would say, "but my daughters deserve nobler hearts."

A stranger, who arrived in the city one day, boasted that he could win the heart of the Emperor's youngest and most beautiful daughter. Everyone who heard him laughed in disbelief. The man was old, ugly and fat. His eyes gleamed with the devilry of a sorcerer.

"The Emperor would never let you marry his daughter," they jeered.

But the stranger's smile turned into a sinister grin. "I have many powers and much magic," he replied. "The Princess will be my bride before nightfall."

When the Emperor saw the stranger, he too was amazed that such a man should think of marrying his daughter. "Strange boaster, leave my palace before I send the guards after you," he declared. "I would rather sell my kingdom than let you marry her."

Just then the stranger called for his servant to enter the room. "Bring the gift that I offer the Emperor," he cried.

The servant came in, hauling behind him a life-size wooden horse. It was perfect in every detail, from head to tail. The Emperor and his courtiers scratched their heads in wonder. Then the stranger spoke again: "I will give this horse to you if you will allow me to marry your daughter."

"Ho! Ho!" laughed the Emperor. "What use is a wooden horse to me?"

"It is a magic horse," said the stranger quietly. "I am a magician. This truly wonderful horse can fly."

The Emperor roared even louder. His courtiers joined in and soon the room rocked with the sound of laughter.

The magician took no notice. He walked over to the horse, climbed onto its back and slipped his feet into the stirrups. Then, touching something behind the horse's head, he rode the beast into the air. Everyone in the room gasped as the horse flew over their heads and up into the open spaces of the roof. Swooping, climbing, diving, turning left and right, the horse and the magician put on a fantastic display.

The Emperor stood speechless, staring wide-eyed as the magician flew around and then finally brought the horse to a perfect landing in front of him. "There, o powerful Emperor," said the magician. "My powers are stronger than yours."

The Emperor was enchanted by the horse. At that moment there was nothing in the world that he would rather possess. "You are a worker of wonders," he told the magician.

"I would give you anything for that horse."

The magician knew what he wanted. "Your youngest daughter in marriage would be a fair bargain," he declared triumphantly.

The Emperor, to everyone's horror, did not hesitate. "Your wish is granted."

The young Princess, who had been watching the proceedings from behind a curtain, was horrified. She ran to the Emperor and begged him to change his mind. "You would give me in marriage to this ugly and evil magician . . . all for a wooden horse?" she sobbed.

But the Emperor was in the grip of the magician's power. He was determined to have the horse. "Daughter! You will obey my command and marry this man."

The Princess ran to her brother, the Prince. "Brother, save me," she cried. "The magician has bewitched our father."

The magician saw that the Prince could be a danger to his plans. "Come, handsome Prince, take a ride on my horse," he said, "and see the magic for yourself."

The Prince decided it would be the best way to discover the secrets of the mysterious wooden beast. He climbed onto the horse and settled himself in the saddle. The magician stepped forward and pressed a small button on the horse's neck.

Instantly the flying horse bore the Prince into the air. Yet this time it did not turn, swoop or dive. The horse flew straight as an arrow towards an open window.

The Prince looked down in panic. "Bring me back," he shouted to the magician, whose face now showed an evil sneer.

The horse and the Prince flew upwards and onwards, through the window and out into the sky. The Emperor could only look on helplessly as his beloved son vanished out of sight.

"Magician!" he roared. "Bring my son back to me at once unless you want the pain of a thousand tortures."

"It is too late," answered the magician. "He flew off before I could tell him how to operate the horse. I fear you will never see him again."

The Emperor called for his guards. "O evil one, you will pay for this mischief," he cried.

The magician pleaded for his life. "I will bring you another magic horse," he shrieked. "Would you not rather have a magic horse than a son?"

"Villain! Vile wizard!" thundered the Emperor, realising that his selfish greed to own the horse had lost him his son. "My son is worth a thousand of your horses. You will rot in a dungeon until my son returns."

The magician was bound in chains and carried away. A damp and dark cell, deep beneath the palace, was his destination. There would be no wedding feast for him that night. Hungry rats would be his companions instead of bridal guests.

The palace was a sad place as night fell. The Emperor cried for his lost son and the Princess wept for her dear brother, who had saved her from marrying the magician. They both sat on the palace roof all night, searching the starlit skies. The moon rose but still there was no sign of the Prince and the horse.

Now, if their eyes had been strong enough, they could have seen him. Far above the palace, beyond the moonlit clouds, the Prince was flying higher and higher. No birds had ever flown so high. The freezing wind rushed past the Prince's ears and, the higher the horse flew, the faster it seemed to go.

'I shall freeze to death,' thought the Prince, hanging onto the horse's head for his life. 'If I do not freeze to death, I shall die by bumping my head on the moon.'

Indeed, the moon was rushing closer as the horse sped through the night sky. 'I must do something,' thought the Prince. 'If there is a button to make the horse climb, there must be another to make it come down, and yet another to make it slow down.'

Gripping the horse with his legs and holding on with one hand, the Prince began to search. 'Allah, be kind to me,' he prayed. 'Help me to master the magic horse.' The horse raced on towards the moon. The Prince searched desperately for a way to slow down the flying beast.

"What's this?" he cried. His hand had found a button behind the horse's left ear. He pushed it and the beast turned to the left and began to descend.

Now the Prince had another problem. The horse was still travelling very fast and in the distance the Prince could see a mountain. He was heading straight for it at terrific speed. He reached for another button. The mountain was quickly approaching when he found a button behind the horse's right ear. A push on this made the horse veer to the right just in time to avoid crashing into the rock face. But they still headed downwards at great speed.

'I can turn left and right,' thought the Prince, 'but where is the button to slow down?' They hurtled on as he desperately tried to find another button. Forests and meadows were

rushing to meet him . . . but then, yes, there it was, another button hidden at the point of the saddle. The Prince pushed it and at last the horse slowed and levelled off in flight. The horse scraped the topmost branches of the trees as the Prince brought it under control.

Now the Prince could relax and he began to experiment with all the buttons. Soon he became master of the horse. He could turn left or right, climb up, come down, go faster or slower when he wanted.

"O magic horse," cried the Prince, "you are not such a devilish beast after all. Come, let us search the skies together." All day the Prince soared through the air. How he enjoyed himself. He raced with the birds, swooped down to scatter the cattle in the fields and glided over the tree-tops.

It was getting late when the Prince's thoughts finally turned to journeying home. But where was he? He examined the ground beneath him. He did not recognise anything he saw as night began to darken the land.

Princess Sheherezade interrupted the story at that point.

"You must not stop there," begged King Shabriar. "I must know what happens to the Prince. I shall die with curiosity if I do not find out."

And so, the next night, the Princess finished the story of The Magic Horse . . .

2 The Adventures of the Prince

The Prince found himself far from home riding the skies on a magic flying horse. He spotted lights glinting in the distance. He turned the horse and flew towards them. Soon he found himself over a small city. The brightest lights shone from a palace and the Prince dropped down towards it. He landed on the roof.

'I will rest here awhile and then try and find my way home in the morning,' he decided. 'I wonder who lives here?'

The Prince dismounted and began to explore. He found a door which led from the roof into a long corridor. At the end of it stood another door. Slowly he opened it. There, on a huge and comfortable cushion, lay a girl. She was fast asleep, her long black hair cascading across the cushion and down onto the floor.

The Prince stared at her face. "Why, she is the most beautiful girl I have ever seen," he whispered under his breath.

He was still looking at her when she awoke. "Who are you?" she asked, very surprised to see the handsome stranger by her bed. "Where have you come from?"

"O beautiful one, do not worry," said the Prince. "I am the son of the Emperor of Persia. I have lost my way and I came by accident on your palace. I must rest before I return home. But where am I?"

"I am a Princess," the girl replied. "My father is King of the Indies. You are a long way from home."

Now, it was a very strange thing, but as the Prince and his new-found Princess looked at each other they fell instantly in love.

The Prince told her all about the magic horse, not that the Princess believed him at first. "A magic horse?" she smiled. "You cannot be telling the truth."

"Come with me," said the Prince. "I will show you. We will ride across the skies to my father's palace and there we will marry."

The Princess was a mischevious young girl at times. She was sure her father would never let her marry the Prince. "If you really do have a magic horse," she told the Prince, "then I will fly away with you." The Princess still did not believe the Prince's story even when she was seated on the horse behind him. But she squealed with delight when it lifted gently off the roof.

The palace was soon far beneath them. The Prince pushed the button on the saddle and, following the sinking moon as a guide, flew at such a speed that they were back in Persia before the sun had crept above the horizon the next morning. The Prince was pleased to see his father's palace again, but he did not land there. He flew the horse to a small village outside the city.

"Fair Princess," he said, "I will run to the city to tell my family what has happened. Then I will send a servant to bring you to my father's palace. Wait here and look after the magic horse for me."

The Prince raced to the city. Emperor Sabur and all the family were delighted to see him again. The Emperor was so pleased that he forgave the magician and freed him from his dungeon.

But the scheming magician was not

50

finished yet. He heard that the Princess was waiting in a nearby village.
Even as the Prince was ordering a servant to go to her, the magician was
sneaking through the city gates.

He reached the village and quickly spied the Princess and the magic
horse. "The Prince has sent me to escort you to the palace," he lied.
"The magic horse will take us there."

The Princess suspected nothing. She climbed onto the horse behind
the evil sorcerer and they flew off. Soon they were over the palace. In the
courtyard the Princess could see the Prince. He was waving to her
excitedly. Something was wrong.

She understood all when the magician, instead of going down to land,
turned the horse and sped off over the city and into the distance.

"Where are you taking me?" asked the frightened Princess, thinking
for a second about leaping from the horse. But they were already high in
the air.

"O foolish Princess," cried the magician. "We are travelling to
another country. The Emperor refused me the hand of his daughter. So
now *you* will marry me."

The Princess's deep sobs were carried away in the wind. "I have lost
my Prince and my father and mother, all in one day," she cried.

They flew through the night and into another day. They landed in
a far off land, a country ruled by a greedy Sultan.

It happened that the Sultan and his courtiers and slaves were returning from a hunting expedition when they came upon the magician and the Princess.

"Save me! Save me!" the Princess cried out. "This vile sorcerer has kidnapped me."

The magician tried to scamper away with the Princess but they were soon surrounded by the Sultan's men.

"By Allah, these are strange travellers," said the Sultan, admiring the beauty of the Princess. "What is that wooden horse that you have brought with you?"

"It is a sign of good fortune," answered the Princess, too frightened to reveal its secrets. "Take it as a present. It will make a fine ornament for your palace."

The magician would have sold the horse's secrets for his freedom, but before he could speak, he was bound and taken off to be thrown in another dungeon.

The Sultan took the Princess to his palace and ordered the horse to be placed in his treasure house. He soon forgot all about it.

The Princess thought all her worries were over. "Sultan, you are my kind rescuer," she said. "My father will reward you well."

"He might indeed, my fair Princess," the Sultan said. "But I have other plans. I have saved you from the sorcerer and my price for that is your hand in marriage."

The Princess was heartbroken. "Marry me if you must," she cried, "but I promise I shall weep until I die."

No one had ever spoken to the Sultan in such a way. He was very angry with the Princess and locked her away in a room all by herself. There she cried from dawn to dusk and through the night as well.

Meanwhile the Prince had not given up hope of finding his Princess again. As soon as he saw her fly off

with the magician, he had vowed to search every corner of the world for her. Wearily he travelled to many countries. It was several months before he reached the Sultan's land.

There he met a shepherd on the road to the city. "Good shepherd, I am looking for a Princess who once promised to marry me. She was stolen from me by a magician."

The Shepherd had heard about the strange arrival of the Princess. "Your Princess is even now at the palace," said the shepherd. "She has fallen ill and does nothing but cry all day and night."

The Prince hurried to the city. His spirits sank when he saw how many guards surrounded the Sultan's palace. How could he possibly reach his Princess?

He walked the streets for hours wondering what to do. Then an idea came to him. He returned to the palace and spoke to the Captain of the Guards. "I am a healer," he explained. "I have heard of a Princess who cries all day and night. Tell your mighty Sultan that I can cure her."

When he heard the news, the Sultan quickly summoned the Prince. "She is to be my bride," said the Sultan. "But I must stop her tears first."

"By the faith of Allah, I can cure her for you," said the Prince. "But I need the magic of a wooden horse to help me."

The Sultan was puzzled by such an odd request. "I have never heard of such wizardry," he said, "but I have such a horse and I will bring it to you."

The Prince was delighted when he saw the magic horse again. He placed it in the middle of the palace courtyard and called on the Sultan to bring the Princess.

The Sultan did as he was asked. The Princess could hardly believe her eyes when she saw the Prince and the horse. He put a finger to his lips. "Do not say a word," he whispered.

The Sultan and his courtiers gathered around the horse to watch

53

the miraculous cure. "Now," said the Prince, "the Princess must sit on the horse and I will take my place behind her. Soon she will be happy again."

The Sultan watched closely as they climbed onto the horse. He saw the Prince stretch out an arm and touch a spot behind the horse's neck. Once more the wooden beast took to the air.

"What magic is this?" said the astounded Sultan, thinking it was all part of the cure.

The horse rose higher and higher, reached the roof of the palace and raced off into the warm blue skies above. The Sultan knew he had been tricked. He shook his fist at the disappearing horse and furiously stamped his foot on the ground.

The Prince and Princess, a happy smile on her face once more, flew fast and high all the way back to Persia. They landed in the Prince's city and Emperor Sabur and all his family rushed out to greet them. Never was there such a happy reunion.

Messengers were sent immediately by the Prince to the Princess's father, the King of the Indies. The Prince wanted to beg his forgiveness for running away with his daughter and to ask his blessing for their marriage. In answer, the King and Queen themselves returned with the messengers to Persia. Seeing their daughter now safe, they happily forgave the Prince and so another happy event took place: the Prince and the Princess were married at last.

King Shabriar asked Princess Sheherezade what had happened to
the magician.

"The Sultan was so angry that he had not revealed the secrets of the
wooden horse," said the Princess, "that he had him put to death."

"And what of the magic horse?" said the King.

"Emperor Sabur destroyed it," explained the Princess. "It had caused him
so much worry and nearly lost him his son. So he put an end to its magic."

The King asked whether there was any more to tell about the horse.

"No," said the Princess, "but I have a story about another voyager, called
Sinbad. Shall I tell it to you tomorrow?"

The King said it would please him very much, so the next night the Princess
began her story.

"Sinbad made many voyages to strange places," said Sheherezade, "and he
survived many incredible adventures. This is how he told the stories to me . . ."

The First Voyage of Sinbad the Sailor

My name is Sinbad. I am the son of a rich Baghdad merchant. He left me
a fortune when he died. I soon learned to live like a King. I wore the
finest clothes, gave great feasts in my many houses and bought my
friends precious presents. Never did I worry about how much I was
spending. I lived a grand life for many years. But one day I went to my
treasure chest and found it was empty. Allah, forgive me, I had wasted
all my father's wealth.

What could I do? I decided to become a travelling merchant myself
and sail the seas in search of trade. I spent my last few coins on buying
sacks of nutmeg, ginger, cloves and other rare spices. I packed them
securely in bales and found a ship to take me on my travels.

We set sail from Baghdad early one morning. All my family and
friends came to see me off and wish me good fortune. I wondered when

I would see them again.

We sailed for many days and nights, stopping at small islands to buy and sell cargo. But as we journeyed further we saw no land at all. Then one day when we were far out to sea, we spotted a strange island. Only a few trees grew on it and it had no beach. Nevertheless, our ship dropped anchor and we went ashore.

What an odd island it was. The land glistened like black ebony. I went off to explore while the others lit a fire to cook a meal. No sooner had the flames begun to flicker than something very strange happened. You might not believe this, but the island shuddered and shook.

'What's this?' thought I. 'An island which moves.'

At that moment someone still aboard the ship shouted out in alarm. "Run for your lives! It's not an island. It's a huge fish!"

Upon my life, it was indeed a fish. It had been lying in the shallow water so long that trees had grown on its back. The fire had awoken the great creature and now it was swimming off to deeper waters.

We all ran back towards the ship as fast as we could. Most of the crew reached safety but my exploration had taken me further afield. The fish sank too quickly for me. "Help!" I cried, the water rising over my scampering feet. Slowly I began to sink as the island monster vanished.

"Allah, save me." I cried. Struggling to keep my head above water, I waved frantically towards the ship. But no one saw me. The Captain, fearing I had drowned, had already raised his sails and was putting out to sea. My spirits fell as I watched the ship disappear over the horizon.

"I have been left to drown," I grieved. "This is the end for Sinbad the Sailor." I would have drowned but just then I saw a plank of wood floating past. I swam over to it and clambered aboard. I found I could sit astride the plank, riding it like a horse.

I paddled with my hands for a while but soon darkness fell. I was alone on the black ocean. What a night I spent. My strength was almost gone. I could hardly hold onto the plank. And worse was to come! All night fish nibbled at my toes. I was sure that any moment a big fish would pass by and swallow me in one bite.

But at last dawn signalled a new day and with it came a wonderful sight. There in the distance was an island. Green grass and leafy trees ran down to the water's edge.

'This is no fish pretending to be an island,' I thought, my spirits lifting. The winds blew me towards it and I fell ashore exhausted. I was asleep before I could count how many toes had been nibbled by the fish.

When I awoke I went in search of food. I found some fruit bushes and ate my fill. My strength slowly returned. But what should I do next?

'Where am I?' I wondered. 'Does anyone live on this island? Will I be trapped here forever?' My questions were answered by the sound of horses' hooves. Racing down the beach galloped the finest white mares I had ever seen. All were without riders, except one.

"Help!" I cried. The rider was very surprised to see me. I was so bedraggled that I hardly looked like a man at all.

"Are you a man, a beast or a fish?" he asked. "Who or what are you?"

It did not take me long to convince him that I was a man and in need of help. "I was lost from my ship," I said. "It was only Allah's kindness which saw me safely here. Where am I?"

"You are in the kingdom of Mihrjan," the man replied. "These are the King's horses, which I exercise every day. Come, I will take you to the city."

The man helped me onto one of the horses and we galloped off. When we reached the city I was taken to see the King. He gave me a hearty welcome and I told him my story.

"By Allah, it is a miracle you were saved from the sea," he exclaimed. "The Gods have protected you well."

The King and I became friends and he made me Master of his harbour. There I noted down the names of all the ships which arrived and listed the cargo they brought. As each ship dropped anchor, my hopes rose. I yearned to hear news of my family in Baghdad. But all the ships came from strange and faraway lands.

"O Sinbad," I said to myself, "this will teach you to go to sea."

The weeks passed and I gave up all hope of ever seeing my home again. Then one morning I saw the greatest sight I had ever seen. Into the harbour sailed the very ship from which I had been lost. I leapt aboard and found the Captain.

"It is I, Sinbad," I cried.

But the Captain did not believe me. "You look like Sinbad," he agreed, "but Sinbad is dead. He drowned at sea. I have brought my ship here to sell his bales of goods. Whatever I get for them I will give to his family."

"They are my bales," I said. "You cannot sell them. They belong to Sinbad. And I am Sinbad!" I told the Captain all that had happened to me since the ship had left me behind. I even showed him where the fish had bitten my toes. At last he believed me.

"Sinbad, it is you," he said. "You are the luckiest sailor on the seas." The Captain immediately ordered my bales to be returned to me. I opened one and, choosing the rarest spices from my cargo, took a small quantity to the King as a present for his kindness.

"This is indeed a rare gift," said the King. "It would fetch a great price in the bazaar because it does not grow on our island."

The next day I took all my bales to the bazaar and sold everything I had. My purse was filled with a hundred gold pieces. I was rich again.

I decided it was time to return home. The King was sad to see me go

but he gave me new treasures to take with me: boxes of silks and fine wines. The voyage back to Baghdad passed safely and my family and friends were delighted to see me again.

"We thought you had been drowned at sea," they said.

I sold all the silks and wines. My treasure chest was full again. I bought a huge house. I filled it with treasures and settled down once more to a life of plenty. I feasted every night, gave my friends more presents and soon forgot about all the hardships and dangers of my first voyage. Even my toes healed.

Yet, as the weeks passed, I grew tired of such a luxurious and comfortable life. 'I need adventure,' I thought. 'And, besides, soon my treasure chest will be empty again. I will board another ship and travel to distant lands to find my fortune.' And that is how I came to make my second voyage . . .

"I like this Sinbad," said King Shabriar. "He has a fine spirit of adventure. Did he tell you about his second voyage?"

"He did, my Lord," said Sheherezade.

"You must tell me tomorrow night," said the King.

The next night Sheherezade began: "This is what Sinbad told me about his second voyage . . ."

The Second Voyage of Sinbad the Sailor

"O Sinbad, do not risk another
voyage," warned my family.
"Remember the dangers which befell
you last time. Think what monsters
are lying in wait for you now."

But I, Sinbad the famous sailor,
would let nothing change my mind.
I went to the bazaar and bought
a fresh cargo of spices, herbs and
other precious goods. Finding a ship
bound for the distant Indies, I said
farewell to my family and sailed
away again.

We did not see land for many
weeks. Then one morning we awoke
to find an island close by. Neither the
captain of the ship nor his crew knew
where we were. Being short of food
and water, we went ashore.

What a paradise! Leafy trees grew
everywhere and the grass was as deep
and soft as a feather bed. The flowers
smelled sweetly and huge oranges
and lemons grew on the bushes. The
rivers ran deep with cool refreshing
water. I went off to explore.

It was not long before I felt tired
and lay down on a bed of grass to rest.
"This must be heaven," said I.
"Perhaps I will sleep awhile." I felt
very drowsy with all the sweet smells
in the air. Soon I was fast asleep,
dreaming of my family back in
Baghdad.

When I awoke I wondered where
I was for a moment. It was evening
and the island was silent. Not a bird
stirred, not a leaf on the trees moved.

I climbed to my feet and looked around. I glanced towards the shore.

"My ship! My ship!" I cried in panic. I ran to the water's edge. The ship had sailed away. Even then I could see its distant sails clearly against the sinking sun. "They've left me behind," I sobbed. "I've been forgotten."

I watched as the ship finally vanished from view. "Alone again!" I cursed. "O Sinbad, why did you not stay at home with your friends. Allah saved you once, but this adventure will be the end of you."

I searched the island. Not one human being did I find. The place was deserted. Soon night fell and new terrors filled my head. What dreadful monsters would eat me as I slept. I dozed with one eye open all night and felt very relieved when dawn broke the next day.

I climbed the tallest tree I could find to get a better view of the island. My eye saw something gleaming at the heart of the lonely isle. "A house!" I cried. "It must be a house."

I jumped from the tree and scampered off in the direction of what I had seen. I was sure I would soon find help. But when I reached the spot, I was puzzled. What a peculiar house it was. A circle of wooden branches surrounded a huge, white dome. It rose high in the air.

I walked around it, counting my steps. "A hundred paces," I marvelled. "A big house indeed, yet it has neither door nor windows."

I was still trying to find a way in when the sky darkened and a mysterious black shadow spread over me. I thought a thunder cloud had covered the sun. I looked up and saw that I was in mortal danger.

"Allah, be merciful!" I cried. There above my head was an enormous bird, its huge wings hiding the whole sky. It was coming in to land, and if

64

I was not mistaken, it had chosen my head as the very spot on which to settle.

I trembled as the flying monster descended. "It's a Roc!" I realised in terror. "A bird so large it feeds its young on elephants."

It was then that I understood what the circle of wood was, and the large dome. This was a nest and the dome was the Roc's egg. "Merciful Allah! I am about to be hatched," I cried. But the Roc took no notice of me and landed on the nest, settling on the egg. I was pinned beneath one of the bird's legs. I dared not move. Each time the bird changed position to make itself more comfortable, its feathers tickled me. I pinched my nose to stop myself from sneezing. If it discovered me, I knew I was done for.

Then I realised the bird had fallen asleep and I began to think of escape. I had an idea. Trapped beneath the monster, I began to unwrap the turban on my head. Soon I had a long piece of cloth. I tied one end of it to the Roc's leg and the other I wrapped around my waist. 'This is my only chance,' I thought. 'When the Roc takes off in the morning, perhaps it will carry me to another island.'

I stayed awake all night. In the morning the great bird awoke and stretched its wings. My heart was racing. Flap! Flap! Flap! The beating wings at last lifted the bird aloft. Hanging from the bird's foot, I rose into the air too. The Roc, so strong and powerful, did not notice its terrified passenger.

Together we soared high into the sky. The island below soon disappeared as we flew far out to sea. What a view I had! The whole world was laid out beneath me.

Presently the Roc began to descend. I saw another island. The bird flew towards it and landed. Bump! I saw stars as I hit the ground. Then I decided Sinbad the Sailor had been a bird long enough. I untied myself and scrambled free. Just then I saw the bird's gaping beak dart at something in the undergrowth. I did not wait to see what it was. I ran for my life. I had not gone far when another dark cloud passed over my head.

It was the Roc again. It had taken off with its first meal of the day. A gigantic, writhing serpent hung from the bird's fierce talons. I was relieved to see both Roc and snake disappear out to sea.

I looked around me. 'What place is this?' I wondered. 'What dreadful fate awaits me now?'

The gods did not disappoint me. I was in a deep valley which clearly had no way in and no way out. High mountains surrounded me. I sat down and sobbed again. "I'm trapped. Allah has forsaken me."

Then I noticed how my tears seemed to sparkle. I looked at the ground below me and was astonished to see that it was covered with diamonds. The precious gems lay scattered everywhere.

I realised then where I was. This was the legendary Valley of Diamonds. I had heard great explorers tell of it before. No man had set foot in the valley and come out alive. The story they told was that every diamond was guarded by a giant serpent.

I shivered with fear. But seeing no serpents, I forgot about my troubles for a moment and collected as many diamonds as I could carry. By evening my trousers and shirt bulged with the valuable stones.

I found a cave to hide for the night. There was a huge rock at its entrance. Once I was inside, I managed to roll it across. No serpent could sneak up on me now. I was safe. I settled down to sleep. My eyes were almost closed when I heard a movement at the bottom of the cave. I sat bolt upright and stared into the darkness, dreading what I might see. First two ghostly green lights appeared, quickly followed by several pairs of smaller ones.

"Merciful gods," I shrieked. "They are eyes! It's a serpent and her young." I scrambled to the cave entrance and heaved at the rock. It rolled aside just as the serpent's hissing tongue was whipping at my ankles.

I fled for my life once more. Leaping, falling, rolling, I escaped down the hill to the valley floor. I was still running as fast as my quivering legs would carry me, when I felt something sharp catch my shirt.

"O Sinbad, this is the end," I howled. I was still running, but my feet were not touching the ground any more. I was flying in the air. I turned my head and saw the worst.

It was not a Roc this time but a great eagle. The creature had me firmly gripped in its talons. "O Allah, take my life now," I cried. "A giant Roc tries to crush me, huge serpents chase me and now an eagle will no doubt feed me to its young."

The eagle flew swiftly over the mountains and out to sea. I struggled to free myself from the bird's claws. I would rather have fallen to my death in the ocean than be torn to pieces in a nest of young eagles. But I was held firm.

I saw land approaching once more and prepared to meet my death. The bird swooped lower and lower. I saw its nest. Four hungry beaks pointed to the sky.

Just then I heard a shout. The ground was very close and I felt the eagle's wings jerk. There was another shout and the bird's claws loosened their grip. One more shout and they released me. I tumbled through the air.

'What now?' I thought as I fell to earth. 'Perhaps an elephant will roll on me.' But there was a surprise in store for me. I fell straight into a thick, leafy bush. Standing beside it was a man, looking at me with very surprised eyes.

"Mysterious traveller, who are you?" he asked, as I climbed out of the bush realising that it was the man's shouts which had frightened the bird into dropping me.

"I am Sinbad the Sailor," I replied proudly. "And this, I hope, is the happy end of my adventures." I told the man my story and he was truly amazed.

"You are indeed a lucky man," he said. "No one has ever escaped from the Valley of Diamonds."

Diamonds! I had forgotten all about them. I emptied my trousers and shirt. My huge collection of diamonds was safe. The man stared at the glittering pile.

"What jewels," he cried. "A king could not be richer."

At that moment I was more interested in finding my way home. "You shall have half of the diamonds if you can find a ship to carry me home," I said.

"It is easily done," he replied. "I am the captain of a ship visiting this island. We sail tomorrow. You will journey with us."

So I set sail for home again. On the way I traded my diamonds at many different islands. I was a rich man again. My family and friends welcomed me home and when they heard of my adventures, they made me promise never to set to sea again. I happily agreed and for many months I lived a splendid life in Baghdad. I became famous for my adventures and many important people came to feast with me and hear my stories. I grew lazy and fat.

Yet slowly, day by day, I grew uneasy and yearned to travel again. My family tried to persuade me against such folly, but I had already forgotten about the terrors of the Roc, the serpents and the eagle.

"That is a good tale," said King Shabriar. "Tell me, did Sinbad ever go to sea again?"

"He did, my King," replied Sheherezade. "He made a third voyage which was as eventful as the others."

"Then you must tell me about it," said the King.

"With your leave, your majesty, I will tell you tomorrow night," said the Princess.

The next night she began her tale: "This is how Sinbad described his third voyage . . ."

The Third Voyage of Sinbad the Sailor

I, Sinbad the Sailor, left behind all the comforts of my life in Baghdad. I said farewell to my family and friends and boarded a ship bound for foreign lands.

We voyaged to many islands, buying and selling goods. I traded my cargo well and earned many gold coins. 'Allah is with me on this voyage,' I thought. 'There will be no creatures to attack me and terrify me out of my wits.'

Ho! How wrong could I be? One morning a violent storm blew up when we were far out to sea and many miles from land. The winds roared and the waves crashed over the decks. The ship was at the mercy of the storm for days. We drifted where the violent wind blew us. Where we would end up, nobody knew.

Not a speck of land did we see for a week, and when the storm finally blew itself out, we were totally lost.

The next day we were delighted to see land ahead. It was not long before we dropped anchor in the beautiful island cove. "Where are we?" I asked. Nobody knew. Just then I saw strange faces looking at us from between the thick bushes which lined the shore.

The captain had seen them too. "Allah, preserve us!" he cried. "I have heard of this place before. It is the island of the Ape Men!"

We quickly saw the trouble we had found for ourselves. Hundreds of the apes, half man and half beast, swarmed onto the beach and into the water. They swam to our ship and boarded us. There was nothing we could do. There were too many of them to hope to defend ourselves.

They grunted and snorted. No one could understand a word they said. But we understood when they pointed to the shore. They wanted us to leave the ship. We dared not argue with them and every man of us jumped over the side and swam to shore.

We reached the beach and turned to look back. Dragon's teeth! The cunning beasts had raised the ship's anchor and set sail. The Ape Men had stolen our ship.

"O Sinbad," I cried, "what dangers have you put yourself in now?" We had no ship and we were stranded on the dreaded Isle of Ape Men, a place no other sailor would dare come near. We were doomed to spend the rest of our lives on the island.

There was nothing to do but explore the island. We were very frightened and kept close together as we cut our way through the heavy undergrowth, expecting to be jumped upon at any second by hordes of Ape Men. But none did we see. Instead we came upon a very strange sight.

A great wall blocked our path. This was no ordinary wall. It was built

of the biggest rocks I had ever seen and rose high into the sky. It would have taken us a week to climb over it. Who could have built such a high wall? And what dreadful secret lay behind it? It was not long before we found out. Walking along the wall for a while, we came on a gatehouse. The two massive doors were open. Seeing no one was about, we walked in.

We stared in amazement. A long and winding path led away into the distance, where a great gloomy castle stood on a hill. It was so huge its walls were half hidden in the clouds.

What were we to do now? We were still thinking about that when the ground began to tremble and shudder.

Thud! Thud! Thud! It was the sound of footsteps. But what footsteps! What creature could make such a terrible noise?

Suddenly, high above the tops of the trees behind us, a huge head loomed. We shuddered at the sight of it. It had but one fiery eye in the middle of its forehead, great teeth which gleamed like fangs and a gaping mouth which could have swallowed all of us like crumbs.

The head had a body too. The trees parted and a monstrous Giant appeared. No wonder the ground shook beneath his feet; the Giant's legs were as thick as tree trunks and his arms its thickest branches.

"Ggggrrrhhh!" bellowed the Giant when he saw us. We were frozen to the spot. A dark shadow swept down on us as the Giant's hand swooped out of the sky and gathered us all up in one snatch. His hand closed around us just like a prison. Looking between the gaps in his fingers, we saw that he was taking us to his castle.

It would have taken us half a day to walk to the castle. But the monster reached it in just a few strides. We heard the castle gates slam behind us and then the hand released us, sending us flying through the air. We tumbled to the ground. We were in the castle courtyard and the gates barred any escape.

We lay where we had fallen, looking up in terror at the Giant. His single eye peered down.

"O Allah, save me," I cried, as the eye settled on me. The Giant's hand reached out and picked me up between two fat fingers. The next thing I knew I was rolling in the palm of his hand, being examined by the hideous eye. The Giant was looking for his next meal.

O lucky Sinbad! He was not to be bothered by such a tiny crumb as me. I was thrown aside and sent flying into a prickly bush.

Then he chose another man to examine. Poor fellow, he was a well-fed man and much more to the Giant's taste. The horrible ogre swallowed the man in one go. The meal seemed to please the Giant. He lay down, took off his great boots, grunted contentedly and closed his eye. Soon he was asleep, great snores echoing around the castle walls.

At that moment I wished I had never left home. I fully expected to end my days in the Giant's stomach. Surely he would eat me when he awoke. I promised myself that if a miracle happened and I escaped from the castle, I would never, never, never go to sea again.

But escape? What hope did any of us have? I looked around the castle yard for an idea. My eyes came to rest on the Giant's boots. A thought came into my head. "I wonder," I said to myself, "I wonder if Sinbad the Sailor could fool the Giant?"

I beckoned to the others to come over. I whispered my plan to them. They agreed it was our only chance. "Come then," I said excitedly. "Let us begin."

We took hold of the laces hanging from one of the Giant's boots and began to heave. The boot was very heavy, but slowly we dragged it closer to the castle gate. At last it was in the position I needed.

I told the others to stand aside while I went and stood beneath the gates. The boot lay between me and the Giant. Then I began to stamp and shout. I made a furious noise and it was not long before the Giant's eyelid began to flicker. The eye opened.

The Giant saw me immediately. He grunted and roared and then clambered sleepily to his feet. My legs shook as he began thudding towards me. My plan was working so far, but the most dangerous part was yet to come.

'Will he see the boot or not?' I wondered. Who knows whether he saw it. It was big enough, but perhaps the sleepy Giant was so angry at being woken that he was blind to everything but Sinbad, his tormentor.

The Giant ran straight into the boot. He tripped and fell. I dodged to the side as the giant crashed to the ground, his head bouncing against the gate. It was exactly what I had hoped for. The gate burst open and the Giant slumped to the ground unconscious. Our escape route lay open at last.

We fled for our lives, running through the gate and onto the path which led to the woods. Looking back we could see that the Giant was

beginning to recover. He was trying to get to his feet.

"Quick," I shouted to my companions. "We must build a raft and escape from this dreadful place."

As soon as we reached the wood, we collected large logs and rolled them to the beach. We cut vines from the undergrowth to use as rope. Lashing the logs together, we built our raft.

Hardly had we tied the last knot, than we heard the roar of the Giant and the sound of his footsteps crashing into the wood. We hauled the raft to the water's edge and launched it to sea. We hurriedly clambered aboard.

Just then the Giant stumbled out of the wood onto the beach. This time he was not alone. Behind him came a Giantess. She must have been his wife. She was as big and as horrible as he.

We paddled for our lives. I thought we were safe. But then the Giant and his wife stooped down and gathered rocks from the beach. Soon a storm of stones and rocks hailed down on us. One by one my companions were hit. They tumbled into the water and vanished. I paddled on, expecting to be thrown into the sea at any moment.

But, Allah be praised, at last I was so far out to sea that even the Giant could not reach me. He raised his arm in fury and roared. Then slowly he and his wife turned and walked back into the wood.

I was happy to see the last of them but I was still not out of trouble. I was alone again on an unfriendly sea. All my friends were drowned. How could I paddle myself to safety? I was miserable and exhausted. I lay down on the raft and the gentle swell of the sea eventually sent me to sleep. How long I slept, I do not know. But the next thing I felt was a jolt which nearly threw me into the sea.

"Allah be praised!" I cried, not believing what my half-asleep eyes saw before me. "I have bumped into a ship."

Already one of the crew had thrown a rope down. I grabbed it and climbed aboard. That was the most amazing part of my third voyage. When I looked at the captain of the ship, I recognised him immediately.

"Do you not recognise me, Captain?" I said. "I am Sinbad the Sailor."

The captain looked at me with a puzzled eye. "Sinbad?" he said, scratching his head. "I once knew a Sinbad who sailed with me. But he was lost."

"Lost?" I cried.

"Yes," said the captain. "We dropped anchor at the island of the Rocs and Sinbad did not return to the ship. We searched everywhere but we could not find him. We thought that perhaps a Roc had swooped down and flown off with him."

"Ha! Ha!" I laughed. "A Roc did carry Sinbad off. But he survived and I will tell you how." I told the captain all my adventures and he at last realised that I was indeed Sinbad, whom he had left behind on Roc Island.

"Allah, be praised," he said. "I have never known a luckier man."

"This is how my third voyage ended. My cargo was still on board the ship and on the way home I sold it all as we stopped to trade at different islands. When I reached Baghdad again I carried with me a sack of gold coins. My family, who had long given up hope of seeing me again, gave me the biggest welcome ever.

Once again I settled down to a fine life. I swore I would never go to sea again. I had had my fill of islands that swam, birds that flew off with me and giants that wanted to eat me.

"No, by the great God Allah, who has brought me home safe from my fantastic adventures, I will not sail the seas again," said I.

"I wonder if Sinbad kept his word this time," said the King as Sheherezade finished the tale.

"I can tell you the answer," said the Princess.

"Must I wait until tomorrow night?" asked the King.

"You must, if you let me live," she replied.

So, the next night, Sheherezade began, "Sinbad may have wanted to keep his word but, as he told me, there were still more adventures in store for him."

The Fourth Voyage of Sinbad the Sailor

I, Sinbad, the famous sailor, promised my family and friends I would never make another journey. Yet one day the Caliph of Baghdad called me to his palace.

"Sinbad," he said, "you have travelled the seas. I have a task for you." The Caliph wanted me to take some gifts to a king who lived in a distant land. It would be a dangerous voyage, but how could I refuse his request? I found a ship and once more set sail.

I reached my destination safely and delivered the gifts to the King. Then I immediately set off for home. How I prayed to Allah to watch over me and see me safely back.

Alas, Allah did not hear my prayers. We had only been at sea a day when a ship filled with pirates appeared ahead of us. Our ship turned tail and ran for its life. I knelt on the deck and prayed, "O, Allah, save me from the pirates."

Allah was still not listening. The pirates' ship was faster than ours. Soon it was alongside, black-bearded pirates screeching for our blood and waving vicious swords above our heads. There were too many of them for us. They swarmed aboard our ship and we quickly surrendered.

"O Sinbad," I cried to myself, "your head will soon roll across the deck." But they did not kill any of us. The pirates tied us to the masts and put our ship under tow. For two days and two nights the pirates hauled our ship towards foreign lands.

Then an island came in sight. The pirates dropped anchor and, untying us, led us ashore. We were marched to a small city and taken to the market place. Soon a crowd of merchants and shopkeepers gathered around us. I realised then what our fate would be. We were to be sold as slaves.

"O Allah," I cried. "If your ears are shut to my pleas, surely your eyes are open. I, Sinbad the famous sailor and friend of Kings and Caliphs, am being sold into slavery."

Allah had one more joke at my expense. A rich merchant bought me for a piece of silver. Such a famous sailor as I should have fetched a king's ransom. Yet my new master was kind enough. He fed and clothed me as well as any slave.

The first thing he asked me was whether I had any special skills. "Can you use a bow and arrow?" he asked.

Ho! Use a bow and arrow? Was I not the best bowman Baghdad had ever seen? "Master," said I, "my arrow would hit a running mouse at two hundred paces."

The merchant was pleased to hear it. He gave me a bow, a dozen arrows and a large knife. Then he led me off into the forest. We travelled a long way and stopped beneath a huge tree.

"Climb to the top of this tree," said my master. "You must stay there until you see a herd of elephants come by. Take careful aim and kill the one with the biggest ivory tusks. Only return to me when you have completed your task."

He left me alone. I climbed the tree and settled into a comfortable spot between two large branches. There I stayed all night. I saw no sign of any elephants and began to doze.

The next thing I knew it was morning and my ears were filled with a thundering noise. I looked out from the tree and saw a herd of elephants trundling down the hill towards the tree. Quickly I drew out an arrow and placed it in my bow. As the elephants came closer I picked out the one with the largest tusks. I took careful aim. Twang! Whoosh! My skills had not deserted me. The elephant fell dead at the foot of the tree.

I clambered down as the other elephants galloped away in panic. I cut off the elephant's tusks and, putting one over each shoulder, set off back to my master's home. He was delighted at my success and sent me back to the tree the next night. I became a very good hunter and every morning for a week I brought him back a pair of valuable ivory tusks.

Yet, I knew it was cruel to kill the beautiful beasts for their ivory. Allah clearly thought so too, because one morning something extraordinary happened. I was sitting in my tree as usual when the herd of elephants appeared. I took out my bow and prepared to shoot. To my surprise, they began to gallop towards me, charging at the tree in terrifying fashion.

I dropped my bow in fright. It tumbled to the ground, landing just as the bellowing elephants came to a sudden halt in a cloud of dust right beneath me. I was trapped. I looked down. Their waving trunks were pointing at me, Sinbad the elephant hunter. Their big sad eyes seemed to be telling me something.

Just then the King of the elephants, a beast as big as I had ever seen, bellowed loudly. The rest of the herd stepped aside as if by command. He walked up to the tree and swung his trunk around it. Furiously the elephant began to shake the tree. I held on for dear life. But the harder I gripped, the angrier the elephant became. He bellowed even louder and the tree swayed violently from side to side.

My strength gave up and I was catapulted from my lofty position. I flew high into the air and tumbled to earth. I was preparing to hear all my bones crack as I hit the ground.

But amazingly I landed neatly on the broad back of the King Elephant. I was so stunned I just sat there, not knowing what to do. The elephant lifted his head and called to the rest of the herd. He walked off and the others followed. I did not dare leap off for fear of being trampled by the elephants behind us.

The grand procession of elephants marched through the forest and into the mountains beyond. It was late in the afternoon when we reached the crest of a hill. There below was a truly amazing sight. Lying on the ground were piles of great bones and heaps of elephants' tusks. A fortune in ivory lay there.

I quickly realised where the elephants had brought me. "O Sinbad," I cried, "this is where the elephants come to die."

The King Elephant, tears in his big round eyes, bellowed gently and dropped onto his front knees. He was asking me to dismount. I climbed down. No sooner had I reached the ground than the elephant rose majestically. He pointed to the ivory tusks with his trunk and turned away. Slowly he led the procession of elephants back into the forest.

I understood all at last. The King Elephant had brought me there for a special purpose. He was showing me where I could collect plenty of ivory tusks without having to kill any more of his brothers.

"O kindly elephants," said I, "you are surely the wisest and kindest beasts of the forest. I will never kill your brothers again."

I ran back to my master's house to tell him of my discovery. That same day I took him to see the place. "Sinbad," he said, "you have brought me a great fortune. How can I keep you as a slave? From this day you shall be my brother and friend. Ask of me what you will."

"There is one thing you could do for me," I said. "I would like to return home."

The grateful merchant readily agreed to my request. Within a few days I boarded a ship for home. I did not travel empty handed. The merchant gave me a cargo of ivories to take with me.

There were more gifts for me when I reached Baghdad again. The Caliph, so pleased I had returned safely from my journey, rewarded me handsomely with many boxes of valuable jewels.

I went home and settled once more into the life of luxury. Hardly a night passed when I did not feast with friends and tell them about my adventures. My family and friends were so happy to have me home again. And every night I promised them that I would never make another voyage.

King Shabriar laughed out aloud. "Ho! What an adventurer Sinbad the Sailor was," he cried. "But tell me Princess, did he ever make another voyage?"

"You heard what Sinbad said," answered Princess Sheherezade. "He vowed he would never go to sea again."

"I do not believe him," smiled the King. "I'm sure he tired of his life of luxury in Baghdad and sailed away again."

The Princess laughed in return. "O wise King, you speak the truth. Sinbad made three more voyages, seven in all. He had many more adventures and became the richest merchant in Baghdad. He lived out his life in great comfort, never ceasing to tell people of his famous travels."

"And now," said the King, "have you another story to tell?"

"I can recall a strange story from the animal kingdom," she said.

The King loved animals and begged her to tell the tale. And so, the following night, Princess Sheherezade began the story of the Wolf, the Fox and the Crow . . .

The Wolf, the Fox and the Crow

There once was a fierce wolf who lived at the heart of the forest. He was master of all the creatures who lived around him. His cruelty was famed and the other animals were frightened of him. Rabbits scampered for cover when they saw him approaching, and mice hid behind rocks as he passed.

The fox also lived in terror of the wolf, who was particularly unkind to the fox, never missing a chance to kick, scratch or bite him. The fox had a very unhappy life. But one day he had an idea. Gathering up all his strength, he went to see his old enemy.

The wolf glared when he saw the fox approaching. "Fox," he said, "you are very brave or very foolish to cross my path."

"O wolf, powerful one of the forest," said the fox, "I would like to speak with you."

"Speak very quickly," barked the wolf, "you are not good to eat but I can still kill you."

The fox trembled a little but went on with his plan. "The forest is very dangerous," he said. "It is full of traps and pits which men have laid down to catch us. If you were my friend I could be your guide through the forest, making sure you do not fall into any of the traps."

"What!" roared the wolf. "You be my friend. You are just a lowly fox and I am Master of the Forest."

At that the wolf lashed out at the fox, sending him tumbling head-over-heels into a bush. The fox lay panting, his side aching. "I only came to warn you about the dangers," he said feebly.

The wolf thought for a moment. If the fox walked in front of him when he went hunting, he would never fall into any traps. The fox would show him where they were by falling in first.

"Fox," he said, "you will never be my friend. But I am going hunting and it might be a good idea for you to go ahead and warn me of any dangers."

"Yes, great wolf," replied the fox. "I will do anything you ask."

The fox walked off through the forest. The wolf followed close behind. He held his head high in the air, sniffing for any scent of something to eat. He did not give a thought to the traps because he knew the fox would fall in first.

The fox may not have been as strong and powerful as the wolf, but he was cunning. They reached a clearing in the forest and the fox looked at the ground and recognised the work of a man. 'There is a pit here,' he thought to himself. 'It is covered by twigs and leaves, but it is surely a pit.'

The fox looked behind him and saw that the wolf was following with his head still held high in the air. He was not looking where he was going. The fox carefully stepped around the hidden pit. Once on the other side he called to the wolf. "All is safe. Follow me."

92

The wolf trotted on. "If the wood is filled with traps," he said, "why haven't you fallen into one yet?"

The words were hardly out of his mouth when the twigs and leaves gave way beneath his feet. The wolf let out a ferocious howl as he crashed through the trap. For a moment his front paws held onto the side of the pit and he tried to scramble out. But the earth around the top gave way and the wolf fell to the bottom.

The fox ran gleefully to the edge of the pit and looked down. The wolf was not dead, just shaken and bruised. He growled and began to jump at the walls. It was no use. They were too steep and the hole too deep. The wolf was trapped.

"Fox!" cried the wolf. "Help me. Run for help. Find something to pull me up."

The fox grinned. "O Master of the Forest, how powerful are you now?"

The wolf grew very angry. He tore at the side of the pit with his paws and snarled viciously at the fox. "Go for help now or I shall kill you when I get out."

But the fox was not scared of the wolf any more. "You will never get out. You cannot get out of there without my help and soon a man will come this way and find you. He will surely kill you."

"No! No!" cried the wolf. "Please help me."

"I came to you for help," answered the fox. "I wanted to be your friend and save you from the traps. You kicked me into a bush for my troubles."

The wolf grew quieter. "I have learned my lesson. I know I have been cruel to you and the other animals. Let me out. I will be a kinder wolf in future."

The fox continued to look down at the wolf. "If I let you out now, you would kill me," he said. "Just like the falcon killed the crow."

"What falcon? What crow?" asked the wolf.

The fox told the wolf the story of a falcon which attacked a crow. The injured crow had limped away to safety in a hole beneath a stone. The falcon could not reach the bird.

"Now, wolf," said the fox, "the falcon called on the crow to come out, promising not to harm him."

"What happened next?" asked the wolf.

"The crow trusted him and came out," said the fox. "The falcon did not keep his promise. He sank his claws into the crow and killed him. That's what you would do to me if I helped you out."

"Never!" said the wolf. "I beg your forgiveness for my cruelty and I promise I will not harm you if you free me. Come, you have a long bushy tail. Drop it into the pit and I will climb out."

The fox would not listen. "You shall learn your lesson," he said. "A man will soon be here to teach you."

Those were his final words. He walked off, leaving the wolf to his fate. Not even the pitiful howls of the trapped animal could make him change his mind.

The fox was pleased that he had made the wolf pay for his cruel ways.

He scampered through the forest. Now the wolf had gone, it was a much happier place. But the fox was a little too happy. His normally cunning eyes were not watching where he was going.

"Snap!" The fox walked straight into an iron trap. One of his front legs was caught fast. He howled in agony.

A crow passing overhead heard the fox's cries and flew down to investigate. "Help me, crow," cried the fox.

Now the crow was a wise old bird. "Come now, fox," said the crow. "If I help you, you will kill me. Remember the story of the falcon and the crow."

"I know it well," he replied. "The wolf, the Master of the Forest, is even now in a pit because I would not trust him."

"Then why should I trust you?" said the crow.

"Because I have learned my lesson," he answered, licking his painful paw.

The crow hopped closer. "If I let you out, will you trust the wolf and let him out?"

"I will let him out if you free me," said the fox. The crow, a brave bird indeed, walked to the trap. Forcing his beak between the iron arms which held the fox's leg, he used every bit of strength he had. At last the gap was wide enough for the fox to drag out his injured leg.

"Now," said the crow, "kill me, or keep your promise."

The fox was grateful to the crow for his kind deed. "Come," he said, examining his leg and finding that it was only bruised. "Let us go and free the wolf. I just hope we are not too late."

The fox limped off and the crow followed in the air. They quickly reached the pit. All was silent. 'Oh dear,' thought the fox. 'A man has already killed him.'

He looked over the edge. Much to his relief, the wolf was still there. He was lying quietly, fully expecting the next moment to be his last. The fox was about to speak when he heard the sound of approaching footsteps. A man was coming towards the pit.

"Quick, wolf," cried the fox. "This is your last chance. A man is coming. Promise now that you will not harm me again. Promise that you will be kind to all the forest animals."

The wolf could hear the man's footsteps now. "Yes, I promise all you ask," he replied. The fox turned around and dropped his bushy tail down the pit. Using his paws and teeth, the wolf clambered up. He was free at last.

Just then the man burst from the bushes. The crow took off and the fox and wolf galloped after him. They reached safety in the heart of the forest and stopped. The crow landed beside them.

At that moment the wolf could have eaten the fox or the fox could have eaten the crow. But the two animals had learned their lesson. The brave crow had done a good day's work.

In the days that passed, the crow, the wolf and the fox became good friends. The crow flew out each morning to see if the man was digging new traps. If he saw any signs, he would fly back to warn his new companions. The fox and the wolf would take it in turns to sit beneath the crow's nest at night. If danger lurked, they would bark out in warning.

Most happily of all, the wolf was never cruel again. The Master of the Forest became loved by all in his kingdom.

King Shabriar was pleased the story ended happily. "I felt sure the fox would kill the crow and the wolf would kill the fox," he said.

"They learned to trust each other," replied the Princess. "There is a lesson for all of us in that story."

"Tomorrow," said the King, "you must begin another tale."

The Princess said she had another good animal story.

"You must tell it to me," said the King.

So, the next night, Princess Sheherezade began the story of the Ox and the Ass.

The Ox and the Ass

Abdullah was a wealthy farmer with a wonderful secret. Allah had given him the power to understand the language of the animals.

He listened to the birds chirping about where they would build their nests. Abdullah overheard bees buzzing about the best flowers to use for making honey. He especially loved to listen to the wise old owls talking late into the night and the frogs croaking at dawn.

Abdullah's magical power was a secret to all but him. Allah had sworn him to keep the secret to himself on pain of death. Not even the Ox, who worked in the fields all day, or the Ass, who carried the farmer to market, could have guessed.

The Ox and the Ass lived in the stable. A low wooden fence divided their homes. The Ox's floor was stony and bare. The Ass lived far more comfortably. His floor was covered with a thick bed of clean straw.

One day Abdullah was walking past the stable when he heard the Ox and the Ass talking.

"Tell me, Ass," said the Ox, "why do you have such a comfortable life? I spend every hour from dawn to dusk pulling the heavy plough in the fields. The ploughman beats me with his stick and when I come home at night I have to sleep on a cold, damp, stone floor."

"But you are fed," said the Ass, turning to find a soft spot in his hay to nestle into.

"Yes," said the Ox, "but only on hay from the yard, and most of that is thick with mud. Yet you are given the best oats and left to rest at home all day. The only time you work is when the farmer wants a ride to market."

The Ass thought for a moment. "Yes," he said after a while, "you do live a harder life than me. But I can give you some advice."

"Tell me! Tell me!" said the Ox.

"In future you must be wiser," said the Ass. "I can teach you how to fool the farmer and his ploughman. Tomorrow, when the ploughman comes for you, pretend to be sick. Bellow and cry, roll on the floor as if you were about to die. Leave the hay he brings. Do not eat one stalk."

"But what if the ploughman still pulls me out into the fields to work?" asked the Ox.

"This is what you do," said the Ass. "When you reach the fields wait until he has harnessed you to the plough. Then fall down and bellow and cry again. If you do that, the ploughman will be sure you are ill. He will bring you back to the stable and give you hay to lie on and good food to eat."

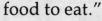

"Your advice is good," said the Ox. "I will do as you say tomorrow." Outside Abdullah smiled as he listened to the animals' plan.

When the sun rose the next day, the ploughman arrived to take the Ox to the fields.

"What's this?" he said, seeing the Ox lying on the ground, bellowing and rolling over and over. "Come, lazy beast, it is time to work." The Ox continued to bellow and refused to eat the muddy hay which the ploughman had brought. The Ox did everything the Ass had said. When the angry man dragged him to the fields, he collapsed between the plough shafts and refused to move. The ploughman beat the Ox as he lay rolling on the ground. Nothing he could do would move the Ox.

'He must be sick,' thought the ploughman at last. 'I will take him back to the stable. He must be kept warm and fed well.'

The Ox was led home. His floor was covered with the thickest hay and he was given the best oats to eat. The Ox winked happily at the Ass. He ate the oats, rolled over in the hay and fell asleep.

Later that day the ploughman went to see Abdullah. "Master," he said, "the Ox is sick. He could not plough today."

Abdullah laughed out aloud. 'So the Ass would teach the Ox bad ways, would he?' he thought. 'If the Ass thinks he can make a fool of me, he had better think again. He will pay for his trickery.' Abdullah turned to the ploughman. "I cannot tell you how I know, but the Ox is not sick. Now this is what I want you to do."

Early next morning the Ox and the Ass were still both fast asleep when the ploughman opened the stable door. Abdullah, not wanting to miss the fun, crept behind the stable to listen to what happened.

"Come, Ass," said the ploughman, clipping him around the ear with his stick. "The Ox is ill. Today you will work in the fields instead."

The Ass blinked in astonishment as the ploughman put a rope around his neck and rudely dragged him to his feet. He was being taken to the fields to work. He began to bray and snort. Abdullah heard what he was saying.

"I am an Ass," squealed the poor animal. "I do not work in the fields. That is the job of the Ox. He is not sick. He is just pretending."

But the ploughman did not have the power to understand animals. "Come with me, you lazy beast," said the ploughman, giving another stinging blow with his stick.

The Ass could see it was no use. His plan had worked against him. He grumbled as the ploughman led him into the fields. He brayed and snorted angrily all the way.

Abdullah roared with laughter as he saw them go. "That will teach the Ass a lesson," he said.

The Ass worked all day pulling the plough. Every time he slowed down, the ploughman beat him. The Ass was not used to such hard work. He was absolutely exhausted at the end of the day. His legs trembled with weariness and he hardly had the strength to stagger home.

He reached home and fell into the stable. The Ox watched in amusement as the Ass slumped to the floor and instantly fell asleep.

When the Ass awoke late that night, he saw the Ox asleep in his comfortable bed of hay. He was furious and kicked the stable door in anger.

"What's the matter?" said the Ox, waking from his slumber.

"I have worked all day in the fields while you rested and ate the best oats," grumbled the Ass. "It's not fair."

"But I only followed your advice," protested the Ox. "I am very grateful to you."

The Ass brayed in disgust and stood sulking in the corner. He was thinking how he could avoid working in the fields the next day. Slowly an idea came to him.

"Ox," he called, "I have another piece of advice for you. It could save your life."

"What!" said the Ox, alarmed. "Tell me!"

"When I was returning from the fields today, I overheard the farmer talking. I heard him say that unless you were well enough to work tomorrow, he could not afford to keep you."

"Is that all he said?" asked the Ox.

"No," smiled the Ass. "He said that if you were still sick tomorrow, he would send you to the butcher to be killed. He said your meat would feed his family for a week and your hide would make shoes for his children."

The Ox bellowed in horror. "The butcher! Oh, help me, Ass. Tell me what to do!'

The Ass was only too happy to give the Ox a second piece of advice. "In the morning you must appear well and lively. Welcome the ploughman and show him you cannot wait to start work again."

"I will! I will!" said the Ox. "The ploughman's stick is better than the butcher's knife."

The next day the Ox did as the Ass had said. The ploughman was delighted to see that he was ready for work and took him off to the fields. The Ox worked so hard he was not beaten once. He pulled his plough faster than ever before.

From that day the farmer and the ploughman treated the Ox with much more kindness. "He has laboured hard over the years," said Abdullah. "He deserves a more comfortable life."

And what happened to the Ass? He returned to his old quiet life. But just occasionally the farmer would tell the ploughman to give the Ox a rest and take the Ass to the fields instead. The Ass never forgot his lesson.

"Understanding animals," said King Shabriar, "that is indeed a fine gift. Some people have difficulty understanding one another even though they speak the same language."

"That is true, my King," replied Sheherezade, "and it reminds me of another man who was understanding enough to marry a tortoise."

"Ah! You must tell me that story tomorrow night," said the King.

The next night Sheherezade began the story of *The Prince Who Married a Tortoise*.

The Prince Who Married a Tortoise

Ali, Husain and Mohammed were the three handsome sons of a mighty King of Persia. When they grew up, the King went to his chief adviser, the Vizier, to seek help in finding each one a princess to marry.

"O Master, it is best to leave it to chance," said the Vizier. "Let them be blindfolded and each shoot an arrow from the palace roof. Where each one lands, let your sons marry the daughter of the nearest house."

The King thought this was a splendid idea and summoned the three Princes, of whom none was stronger, braver and kinder than the youngest whose name was Mohammed. The brothers gathered their bows and climbed to the palace roof.

The first to fire his arrow was Ali. It flew high and far, landing in the garden of a wealthy lord. His daughter was pretty but greedy.

Husain's arrow landed nearer the palace, crashing through the window of the Lord Chamberlain's house. He readily agreed to let his daughter, a beautiful but spiteful girl, marry the Prince.

Mohammed stepped forward and fired his arrow. It flew the furthest of all. Indeed the king had to send out servants to discover where it had landed. They returned with sad faces. "The arrow landed in the house of a tortoise," they said.

"What!" exploded the King. "My youngest son cannot marry a tortoise. Mohammed must shoot again."

Mohammed's second arrow again flew out of sight. The servants went in search and returned with glum faces. "The arrow has landed in the Tortoise's garden again," they said.

The King was amazed and called for Mohammed to fire a third arrow. The power of Allah took it to exactly the same spot in the Tortoise's garden.

Mohammed, always a cheerful young man and ready to accept his fate, took off his blindfold and spoke to his father. "Allah has taken my three arrows to the Tortoise's garden," he said. "It is his will that I should marry her."

"So be it," said the King, who did not want to risk the wrath of Allah.

The three brothers were married soon after. Hundreds of powerful nobles and lords and wealthy merchants came to see Ali and Husain marry their new wives. But none but the King, who loved all his sons dearly, came to the wedding of Mohammed and the Tortoise. He even gave the gentle-faced creature a ring to wear on her flipper.

Ali and Husain and their Princesses moved into huge mansions near the King's palace. Mohammed and the Tortoise went to live in a tiny house on the edge of the city. The Princesses never came to visit. They always said they were too high and mighty for a tortoise's home.

One day the King fell ill. The three Princes hurried to his bedside.

"The cause of his illness is the bad food his servants prepare," said Ali. "In future our wives must cook him special dishes."

"Yes," said Husain, "but how can a tortoise cook fine meals?"

"Don't worry," said Mohammed, "my wife will not disappoint you."

When the Tortoise heard that each of them was to cook for the King, she was delighted. But what a strange way she went about preparing her dish. First she sent a servant to Ali's home to ask his Princess if she had any old bones to spare. The greedy Princess refused to help and sent back a rude message to the Tortoise. The Tortoise did not seem worried at all. In fact she laughed merrily.

Next she sent her servant to ask Husain's Princess if she could spare some lumps of fat. Her answer was the same. But still the Tortoise was not upset.

The Tortoise spent all night working in her kitchen and in the morning her meal for the King was ready. She took it to the palace where the Princesses were waiting with their dishes.

The three dishes, each covered by a cloth, were taken to the sick King. The first to be served was the one cooked by Ali's Princess.

"Devil's trickery!" cried the King, removing the cloth. "A thousand curses on she who cooked this." The dish was piled high with old bones. Ali's Princess was horrified. Her face turned bright red.

Husain quickly brought the dish which his Princess had made. The King was even angrier when he took off the cloth from the second dish.

"Whose mischief is this?" he said. "This cook would kill rather than cure me." The dish was awash with greasy lumps of fat.

The King was furious with the Princesses and banished them from his palace for forty days and forty nights. They left in disgrace, completely mystified as to why their specially prepared dishes had turned into bones and fat.

At last it was the turn of the Tortoise. "If human beings can only give me fat and bones," thundered the King, "what am I to expect from a tortoise?"

The lid on the Tortoise's dish was removed. Delicious smells burst forth and all could see the colourful rice, the dainty meats and the sweet fruits which filled the plate. The King began to eat and he did not stop until every morsel was gone. Then he patted his stomach and smiled in satisfaction.

"You are a wonderful cook," the King told the Tortoise. "You shall prepare all my meals until I am cured."

The Tortoise cooked the King many fine dishes and he soon recovered from his illness. When the Princesses heard what had happened they grew very jealous and wondered how they could win back the King's favour. They desperately wanted to make the Tortoise look bad in the King's eyes.

Their chance came when the kindly King decided to forgive them. He announced a huge banquet to mark the occasion. The Princesses planned to arrive at the banquet in grand style with fine coaches and horses and small armies of richly dressed slaves. "The Tortoise will not be able to match the splendour of our arrival," smirked the Princesses.

But the Tortoise suspected the

Princesses' plot and put her own plans into operation. First she sent her servant to Ali's Princess asking to borrow a goose. The Princess refused. The same happened when the Tortoise asked Husain's Princess for a goat. The mysterious Tortoise was not upset. She just laughed happily.

On the night of the banquet the King and all his courtiers gathered to await the arrival of the Princesses. O, what magic happened that night! Someone had played a mischievous trick on the two Princesses.

The King roared with laughter when he first saw a huge goose waddle into his court. Sitting on its back, and hanging onto its neck, was Ali's Princess. Immediately behind the goose was a goat. Riding upon it was Husain's Princess.

"Oh, I have never seen anything so funny in all my life," laughed the King. "Two Princesses riding on a goose and a goat. I can hardly wait to see what strange beast the Tortoise comes on."

But it was not a tortoise which arrived next. A silver coach drawn by six black stallions galloped into the court. It drew to a stop in front of the King. The door opened and out stepped a Princess whose beauty far outshone that of all the other Princesses.

"Who is she?" whispered the stunned onlookers. "Where is the Tortoise?"

The clever King knew exactly who the Princess was. He had already seen the ring on her finger. It was the very one he had given to the Tortoise on her wedding day.

"If you are the one I think," said the King, "you are most welcome to my banquet."

"Master, I am glad that you recognise me," said the beautiful Princess. "Allah's arrow was true. I am indeed she who married your youngest son Mohammed."

The King was delighted. He sat Mohammed and the Princess at his right side during the banquet. The other two Princesses glared jealously at their rival.

But the magic was not finished yet. When the rice was served, Mohammed's Princess raised the pot and dropped it all over her hair.

Instantly her silky black locks were sprinkled with diamonds. She did the same with the green pea soup. As she poured it, emeralds sprung from her hair.

All the guests clapped their hands in amazement. The other Princesses saw what had happened and, not to be outdone, did exactly the same. They tipped the rice and the soup over their heads.

Oh, how everyone laughed. There were no diamonds or emeralds for them. The rice hung from their hair and the soup dribbled down their faces. They ran from the room in rage. The last anyone saw of them they were being chased through the palace corridors by a goose and a goat.

The story of the Prince who married the Tortoise is almost at an end. There are but two things to tell. The happy couple left their humble house on the edge if the city and moved into a grand palace close to the

King. He loved them dearly for the rest of his life.

   Yet there was one thing he never told them. The day after the famous banquet, the King rode out to the edge of the city to see their old house. He thought he might find something. He was right. There, lying on the floor, was the empty shell of a tortoise.

King Shabriar liked the story of the tortoise very much. "I wonder if Mohammed knew the Tortoise would turn into a Princess," said the King.

"He had faith in Allah's judgement," said Sheherezade.

"Do you have another story to tell?" asked the King.

"I know a tale about a poor ropemaker and two rich brothers," she answered. "If you let me live another night, I will tell it to you."

The King granted her wish and so, the following night, the Princess told the story of Hassan the Ropemaker . . .

Hassan the Ropemaker

Hassan was a kindly ropemaker who lived in Baghdad. He was poor but happy. He loved his wife and children. They were worth more than money to him.

Now it happened that close by lived two rich brothers called Saad and Saadi. They were generous and kind and much liked by everyone. But they had one fault. They could never agree on anything. Saad and Saadi argued from sunrise to sunset.

If one said it would rain that day, the other would insist the sun would shine. If Saad said friends would visit them in the morning, Saadi would say they would come in the afternoon. There was nothing they could agree upon. If the truth was known, Saad and Saadi enjoyed nothing better than an argument.

One day they went to Hassan's shop to buy some rope. They saw how poor he was and began to argue.

"I say that anyone can become rich if someone gives him some money to start with," said Saad. "As long as he uses the money sensibly he will certainly become rich."

Saadi, of course, disagreed. "You cannot make a man rich by giving him money," he said. "He will neither become rich nor happy. Only the grace of Allah can make a man rich."

113

The brothers argued about it all day. At last Saad, seeing that Saadi would not change his mind, decided to settle the matter.

"We will carry out an experiment," he said. "We will see which one of us is right. I will try my way first. If I fail, it will be your turn."

The next day they returned to Hassan's shop. Saad spoke to the poor ropemaker. "You are poor," he said, "and I have plenty of money. Let me give you a gift."

Saad gave an astonished Hassan one hundred gold coins. "Do what you want with it," he said.

When the brothers had left the shop Hassan put the coins in a bag and hid it among the folds of his turban. Then he hurried off home to tell his family the good news. He had hardly gone a few steps when an eagle swooped out of the sky. It snatched Hassan's turban in its beak and flew off with it.

Hassan watched the eagle disappear over the city roofs and fly out of the country. He was surprised but not angry. "Money cannot make me any happier," he said.

The weeks passed and Saad and Saadi returned to Hassan's shop. Saad was disappointed to see that the poor ropemaker was still as poor as ever.

"What happened to the money I gave you?' asked Saad. Hassan explained how the eagle had flown off with his turban and the bag of gold coins.

Saad did not believe him. "Eagles don't snatch turbans. You are lying."

Saadi interrupted. "Hassan is not lying," he said. "He may be poor but he is not a liar. I believe that an eagle did fly away with the money."

Saad stamped his foot in annoyance. "Whatever happened, it has not made him rich," he said. "Now, Saadi, it is your turn to prove your argument that only the grace of Allah will make a man rich."

Saadi said he would be happy to do so. He put his hand in his pocket and pulled out a small piece of lead. "Here," he said to Hassan. "I found this piece of lead on the road. I would be pleased if you would accept it from me as a gift."

Saad could not believe his eyes. "A piece of lead," he laughed. "How can that make a poor ropemaker rich?"

"We shall see," said Saadi.

That night Hassan took the piece of lead home and threw it into a box of other worthless bits and pieces. He forgot all about it and went to bed. He was awoken in the middle of the night by a knock at his door.

Half asleep, he went downstairs and opened the door. It was an old

fisherman friend. "Dear Hassan," said the fisherman. "I am sorry to wake you. I have no food and I wanted to go fishing tonight. But I have no lead weight for my line."

Hassan remembered Saadi's strange gift. "What is a friend if he cannot help?" said Hassan. "I can give you a piece of lead." The fisherman was very grateful and promised Hassan that he would give him the first fish he caught that night.

The next morning the fisherman returned. "I had good luck last night," he said. "I caught many fish. Here, as

I promised, is the first one I caught. May it feed all your family."

Hassan had never seen such a large fish. Nor had his wife. "My stove is not big enough to cook it," she said. "I will have to cut it in two." She took the fish to her kitchen and cut it in half with a knife. "How strange," she cried. "What's this?"

Out of the fish tumbled a large shiny stone as big as a canary's egg. Hassan's wife picked it up and looked at it. "It will be something for the children to play with," she said.

What fun it gave the children. They played with the stone all day. They rolled it like a marble, and threw it as a ball to catch. They even used it as a mirror. It was so shiny that they could see their faces in it.

When Hassan returned that night his wife told him about the stone. He was delighted that his children had something to play with. He could not afford to buy them many playthings. But when he saw the stone, his eyes lit up. "Merciful Allah," he cried. "This is not an ordinary stone. It is a diamond. It is worth a thousand pieces of gold."

Then he remembered Saadi's gift. "The piece of lead has brought me good fortune." Hassan took the stone to market to sell. Indeed, it was

116

worth a thousand pieces of gold. He returned home a rich man. The first thing he did was to reward the fisherman. He gave him five hundred pieces of gold.

Hassan used the rest of the money wisely. He hired other poor ropemakers in Baghdad to come and work for him. His business grew very large and soon he had to open a new and larger shop. It was not long before he became the wealthiest ropemaker of all Baghdad.

He bought a new house in the country and filled it with servants. Like the ropemakers who worked for him, he paid the servants well. Hassan became famous for his generosity.

News of Hassan's sudden wealth reached the ears of Saad and Saadi. They went to visit him, still arguing which of the two had made him rich.

Hassan greeted the brothers warmly, but Saad was still suspicious. "Come, Hassan, now you can tell me the truth," he said. "You invented the story about the eagle, did you not? Surely the money I gave you was never stolen. You used it to become rich."

"I swear I told you the truth," replied Hassan. "Listen. I will tell you the story of the piece of lead and how it made me rich."

When he had finished, Saad said: "Nonsense. I do not believe a word of it." All day he argued with Saadi. He was still squabbling that evening when Hassan took the brothers for a walk in his gardens before feasting. Hassan could not help laughing at how much the brothers argued.

At the bottom of the garden was a small wood. Just as they reached it, Hassan noticed something strange at the top of the highest tree.

"I will leave you to your arguments," he said. "I want to climb this tree to see what lies at the top of it."

It was a long and difficult climb, but at last he reached the top. "By Allah!" he cried. "This is an eagle's nest. Yet what a strange nest it is." He removed the nest from the branch and clambered down to the ground again. "Look what I have found," he said excitedly.

Saad and Saadi looked at the strange object. "It is a nest," said Saad.

"Indeed it is," added Saadi. "But it is also a turban. The eagle has made a nest out of a turban."

Hassan shrieked with delight. "Yes. And do you not see that it is my turban, the very one which was snatched from my head?" The brothers watched as Hassan unwrapped the turban. Out of it tumbled a bag. It clinked with the sound of coins. Hassan opened it and counted out one hundred gold coins.

"O Hassan, can you forgive me?" said Saad. "You spoke the truth all along. It truly was my brother's piece of lead which made you rich."

"Not just the piece of lead," interrupted Saadi, "but Hassan's kindness and the grace of Allah."

That night Hassan and the brothers feasted happily. Saad and Saadi hardly argued at all. There was just one thing though. They could not agree who was now the richer. Was it them or Hassan?

Only Hassan knew the answer to that.

King Shabriar laughed out loud. "Saad and Saadi are like all brothers," he said. "They will always argue."

"Hassan had the last laugh on them," replied Princess Sheherezade. "He did become richer than both of them."

"Hassan became rich, but he also stayed a happy man," said the King. "I would like to hear another story like that."

"I know a story about a man whose nature was changed by riches," said the Princess. "If you wish, I shall tell it to you tomorrow night." The King agreed readily.

The next night Sheherezade began the story of Mohammed Lazybones.

The Tale of Mohammed Lazybones

It was a strange thing that Mohammed Lazybones had such a name for never was there a more hard-working man and nowhere was there a man quite so rich.

He lived in a palace as big as the Sultan's. He sat on a pearl and silver throne and ate and drank only the best food and wine. At night he slept upon a golden bed, covered by sheets of the finest silk. Fifty servants surrounded the bed to keep him cool with great feather fans. The palace walls were studded with priceless jewels, the garden blossomed with the rarest flowers and his treasure house overflowed with precious goods of every kind. Lazybones was the envy of every man.

Yet nobody knew how he had become so rich. "How could a man, once so lazy, become so wealthy?" they said. "Was he not the son of a poor barber?"

Lazybones kept his secret for many years. Then one day he decided to reveal all. He opened the palace gates and announced that he was going to tell his story. Many people crowded inside to hear the tale. This is how Lazybones told it.

My tale is a marvellous one. It may be hard to believe, but it is true. I was the son of a poor barber. When he died he left me nothing but my name. He called me Lazybones and there was a very good reason for this. As a young man there was no one lazier than me. I hardly ever got out of bed. If I did, it was only to lie around the house or in the garden. When I was outside in the sun, I always burned my nose because I was too lazy to move into the shade. If it was really hot my mother would have to move me.

When my father died, my mother had to go to work to earn enough money to feed me. I waited in bed for her to bring me my daily meals. One day, however, she came home very excited. She had been given a gold coin by a kind gentleman.

"Lazybones," she said, "this coin will bring you a fortune."

I was not very interested. I turned over in bed and tried to rest a little. But my mother had made up her mind not to let me be lazy any more.

"There is a rich sheik who is about to sail for China," she said. "Take this coin to him and ask him to bring you back something which you can sell for a profit."

I complained that the harbour was a very long way away. "I shall probably fall asleep on the way," I moaned.

"Lazybones!" she snapped. "I will never bring you another meal unless you get up and run down to the harbour with this coin."

'My goodness,' I thought. 'If my mother does not bring me food, how will I live?' I had no choice. I reluctantly agreed to the idea.

But, being so lazy, I did need a little help. My mother got me out of bed, dressed me, put on my shoes, washed my face and brushed my hair. I did walk some of the way to the harbour,

122

though I have to confess that my mother carried me on her back for most of the journey.

I found the sheik and gave him the gold coin. "Buy me something in China," I said. "Anything that I can sell for a profit here." The sheik agreed to take my money and I called on my mother to help carry me home. I went straight back to bed when I got home. It had been such a tiring day.

I will now tell you what happened to the sheik. He reached China and went about his trade. One morning he was in a market-place when he saw a group of monkeys belonging to a shopkeeper. In the middle of them was a young one, covered in cuts and bruises. The shopkeeper explained to the sheik that the older monkeys bullied and bit the youngster all the time. The sheik was a kindly man and it was then that he remembered my gold coin. He bought the little monkey for me and what a wonderful animal it turned out to be.

On the journey home the sheik stopped the ship so that he and some other rich merchants aboard could go diving for pearls. The monkey watched the men dive overboard and then followed them. It vanished beneath the surface. Everyone on board the ship was sure the monkey would drown, but shortly afterwards it reappeared. There was a big grin on its face and a large bag between its paws. The bag was opened and out tumbled not just pearls, but jewels of every kind. The clever monkey had found treasure on the ocean floor.

The sheik was amazed. "This is the monkey I bought for Lazybones," he said. "So these jewels rightly belong to him."

They continued on their journey home but had not gone far when a band of pirates attacked them. The sheik and the merchants were overpowered and each man was tied up and lashed to a mast.

Do you know what that monkey of mine did? It hid itself until nightfall and then crept out under cover of darkness and untied the sheik. He was so grateful that he vowed to give me a hundred gold coins if he got home safely. He also told the other merchants that it would cost them a hundred gold coins each for my monkey to untie them.

As soon as they were all free, the sheik and the merchants took the pirates by surprise and hurled them off the ship into the sea. Then they sailed for home.

I was in bed when my mother came in and said that the sheik's ship had returned. "You must go down to the harbour to see what they have brought you," she said.

I couldn't be bothered. I had had a busy day lying in bed and was very weary. My mother cursed my laziness. "What will become of you?" she cried.

Just then there was a knock at the door. It was the sheik. Beside him stood the monkey. My mother brought them to my bedside. The sheik did not tell me all at first and I was very rude to him.

"What can I do with a monkey?" I asked. "I would rather you gave me my gold coin back." But then he told me the rest of the story and laid a large bag on my bed. Out of it poured the jewels which the monkey had found and then the hundreds of gold coins which the merchants had paid to be untied on the ship.

I couldn't believe it. 'All this for just one gold coin,' I thought. 'Perhaps this monkey is showing me how much better it is to work than to lie in bed all day.'

I leapt from my bed and let out a great cry. "Mother, I will be lazy no more," I shouted. "I shall become a merchant with the riches the gold coin has brought and send ships all over the world to trade. What is more, my friend the monkey will travel with them and bring me more good fortune."

My wealth grew greater with every voyage. The monkey amazed all who sailed with him and he brought me back many great treasures from distant parts. I bought land, built houses and planted fabulous gardens. There was no limit to my wealth. I became as rich as you see me now.

My story is a strange one, but the monkey's was even stranger. One day he returned from a journey and, as usual, was brought to my palace. No sooner had the treasures of the voyage been laid at my feet than the monkey let out a cry of happiness.

There and then, right before my eyes, the monkey changed into a handsome young genie. I shrank back in surprise and fear. But the genie spoke to me in a gentle voice. "Do not be frightened," he said. "I have much to thank you for."
I couldn't imagine what he had to thank me for.

"I was once a very lazy genie," he explained. "My gods punished me and turned me into a monkey. Never could I become a genie again unless I found a lazy man and made him rich and hard-working. This I have done. You are now rich and cured of your laziness."

I wanted to thank him for making me so rich. But he must have been in a hurry to get back to his own world. He waved an arm and in a flash he had flown through an open window and disappeared into the clouds beyond.

There ends the story of how I, Mohammed Lazybones, became one of the richest men of all. If my father came back to life now, I wonder if he would still call me Lazybones.

"So, Mohammed's nature was changed by his wealth," said the King.

"Yes," said the Princess. "Of course there are many different kinds of wealth that can change someone's nature."

"You mean love and happiness, for example. I see you are talking about me," said the King, smiling.

"That reminds me of another story," said Sheherezade. "It is about a poor boy whose life was changed by the chance of great riches. His name was Aladdin."

"You shall tell me the story tomorrow night," said the King.

Aladdin and the Wonderful Lamp
1   Aladdin and the Cave

Aladdin was the son of a poor Chinese tailor. The tailor died when the boy was very young and Aladdin's mother did her best to feed them both from what little money she earned spinning cotton.

One day Aladdin was playing with his friends in the market-place when a strange figure in a black cloak appeared. His half-hidden eyes glinted from beneath a dark hood.

The stranger approached Aladdin. "Young man," he said, "I have travelled all the way from Africa to see my brother, your father. And Allah has been unkind. I hear my brother is dead."

Aladdin didn't even know he had an uncle. The stranger took two objects from his pocket. One was a ring, the other a gold coin.

"Put on this ring, nephew," he said, "and take this gold coin. I am going to make you rich." Aladdin couldn't believe his good fortune. "Now come with me," said his uncle. "I want to show you something. It's not far." They walked out of the city and stopped at the foot of a huge mountain.

"This is the place," said Aladdin's uncle. "Now go and collect some firewood." Aladdin did as he was told and soon had a fine bundle. His uncle took out his tinder box and made a fire. Aladdin was very puzzled as to why he should want to light a fire on such a hot day. But just then his uncle took out another small box and sprinkled powder on the blaze. Whoosh! A column of smoke burst from the fire and the mountain shook. Aladdin jumped backwards as a huge pit opened up in the ground by his feet.

"By Allah, you are a magician, uncle," cried Aladdin, trembling and looking fearfully at the great gaping pit below him. He saw that the bottom was covered with a shiny marble slab. A brass handle was fixed in the middle of it.

"This is our path to riches," said Aladdin's uncle. "It is a magical place, full of great treasures. We will share them together."

"So you *are* a magician," said Aladdin.

"You might call me that," he replied, a cruel grin creeping across his face. "I learned many things in Africa and my magic revealed to me this place. Yet my magical powers told me that it would be death for me to enter it. That is why I have brought you. Only one person may enter, and you are the chosen one. Now, climb down and open the great stone by pulling on the brass ring."

Aladdin was frightened. "That stone is too heavy for me," he said. "I could never lift it."

His uncle grew angry. "Do not disobey me or Allah will punish you. Jump into the pit now and pull up the stone."

Aladdin, fearing his uncle might hit him, jumped down and took hold of the ring. Much to his surprise, the stone lifted easily, revealing some steps leading down to a door.

"Now listen very carefully," said his uncle. "Go through that door and

you will find yourself in a large cavern. You will see that it is full of barrels, overflowing with gold."

"Shall I bring the gold to you?" asked Aladdin.

"No!" said his uncle sharply. "Ignore the gold. Walk through the cavern and you will come into a garden with trees. Follow the path through them and you will see a wall. Standing on it will be a brass lamp. That is what you must bring back to me. Do you understand?"

Aladdin shivered again and said he understood. The fierce look on his uncle's face told him it was time to go. He went down the steps slowly and opened the door. The cavern behind it was indeed packed with barrels of gold.

"I could be as rich as a king," whispered Aladdin. But fearing his uncle's anger, he did not stop. He walked on past the golden treasures and came into the garden. It was thick with trees. Yet something was very odd about them. The fruit on the branches hung like shining stones. Just then Aladdin saw the wall at the end of the garden. There on top of it stood an old brass lamp.

"How odd that my uncle should want this lamp, rather than the gold," said Aladdin to himself. He climbed some steps to the wall and took

hold of the lamp. Safely putting it inside his shirt, Aladdin set off back.

He had not gone far when the fruit on the trees attracted his attention again. "I shall just take a pear," said Aladdin. He plucked a pear from the nearest tree. "Ha!" he said, very surprised. "This is no pear." Indeed it was not, it was cold to touch and as hard and shiny as glass. "Never mind," he said. "These glass fruits are beautiful. I will gather some and give them to my friends." He quickly stuffed his shirt full of the fruits and ran off back into the cavern. He passed the gold barrels and climbed up the steps.

He was met by the fierce eyes of his uncle, looking anxiously down into the pit. "Hurry, give me the lamp," he snapped.

"I cannot," said Alladin, "I must take out all the fruits I collected first."

His uncle grew angrier. "Do not disobey. Give me the lamp this minute!"

"Uncle, please give me a hand and pull me up," said Aladdin. "Then I can give you the lamp."

"No!" roared his uncle, angrier than ever. "You will stay there until you have given me the lamp."

Aladdin saw for the first time the evil look in the stranger's eyes. 'This is no uncle of mine,' he thought. 'He is a sorcerer who has used me for some mysterious purpose.' He saw the stranger disappear from the top of the pit for a moment and then return. He had a large stick in his hand.

"Come here this instant and give me the lamp or I shall beat the life out of you!" he shrieked. Aladdin ran back through the door into the cavern.

"You are not my uncle. You are a sorcerer!" he cried, his head peeking out from behind the door. "I will not come out."

The stranger ranted and raved at Aladdin until the sun had set. But Aladdin would not move. He knew he was safe in the cavern. After all, the stranger had told him it was death for him to enter it.

"If I cannot have the lamp," hissed the sorcerer finally, "then no one will have it. Death to Aladdin."

The stranger lit the fire once more and took the box of powder out of his pocket again. Taking a pinch of the magic powder in his fingers, he threw it on the flames. Whoosh! The mountain shook once more and the pit in the ground vanished in a puff of smoke.

Looking up, Aladdin saw the great stone crash shut above his head. He cried out in terror. "Uncle! Uncle! I will give you the lamp. Let me out!"

It was too late. The sorcerer had done his work. He was already setting off on his long journey back to Africa. "The cavern will make a fine tomb for Aladdin," he snarled. "He has robbed me of the lamp and it will cost him his life."

Deep beneath the ground, Aladdin sat shivering in total darkness. Tears

132

streamed down his face. He began to wring his hands in misery. As he did so, he rubbed the ring on his finger, the one the sorcerer had given him when they first met in the market-place.

Whoosh! Suddenly the cavern was lit by a bright light. Aladdin blinked in astonishment as he found he was no longer alone. A genie had appeared from the ring in a puff of smoke. Aladdin was struck dumb with surprise. Black of face and a multi-coloured turban on his head, the genie had eyes that gleamed as brightly as his big shiny teeth.

"O, Master, I am the Slave of the Ring," boomed the Genie. "Your wish is my command." Aladdin was confused and the Genie spoke again. "By rubbing the ring you bid me to come to you. O Master of the Ring, what can I do for you?"

Aladdin began to understand at last. Clearly the sorcerer had given him the ring not knowing its powers. "If I am Master of the Ring, then so be it," said Aladdin. There was only one thing he wanted and did not hesitate to ask. "Free me from this cavern."

"Your wish is my command," said the Genie. In an instant Aladdin found himself standing outside on the very spot where the pit had been. The Genie had vanished.

Aladdin was sure he was dreaming. Then he saw the fire which the sorcerer had lit. "So this really did happen," he said. "I must hurry home in case the sorcerer appears again."

He ran home and told his mother the whole astonishing story. She didn't believe one word of it.

"I can prove it," said Aladdin. "Look at the ring on my finger. Look at the glass fruits I have brought back. And look at the lamp." Aladdin produced his collection of fruits and laid the lamp beside them. "There. This is the lamp which the sorcerer would have killed me for," he exclaimed.

"Why should he kill you for that lamp?" puzzled his mother. "It is worth but a few potatoes, and those fruits would not buy a tomato. You can sell them all at the market tomorrow."

"I think there is more to that lamp than you have told," said the King.

"It is late now," replied Sheherezade.

"Then you must continue tomorrow night. I am sure we have not heard the last of that sorcerer either," said the King.

"I shall reveal the answers if you are patient," said the Princess.

The following night Sheherezade continued the story.

2 The Magic Lamp

"Come, Aladdin," said his mother next morning. "Go to the market and sell the lamp. It will buy us food. Let me polish it before you go. It will be worth more." Aladdin's mother took the lamp into the kitchen and found a cleaning rag. She began to polish the old lamp.

Whoosh! A puff of smoke burst from the lamp and out of it jumped another Genie. He was huge. He sat cross-legged on the floor, but his head still touched the ceiling.

"I am the Slave of the Lamp," thundered the Genie. "Your wish is my command," Aladdin's mother was so surprised she fainted to the floor. Aladdin, hearing the noise, ran in.

"By Allah, another Genie," he cried.

"I am the Slave of the Lamp," the Genie repeated. "Your wish is my command."

"Slave of the Lamp," said Aladdin. "I am hungry. Bring me a fine feast."

The Genie vanished and then appeared with a huge tray. It was covered with solid gold and silver plates overflowing with the most delicious food. The Genie bowed to Aladdin and disappeared.

When Aladdin's mother recovered, Aladdin explained the mysteries of the ring and the lamp. "Come, mother, let us eat."

She was still too frightened to eat. "Aladdin," she said, "you must sell the ring and the lamp. They will only bring us trouble."

Aladdin said he could not sell the ring because it had saved his life. But he promised to hide the lamp so that she would never see it again. "Neither will bring us bad luck," he said. "You will see."

Aladdin hid the lamp in a space behind a loose stone in his bedroom. "I shall not need this," he said. "In future I can sell the gold plates the Genie brought to buy us food."

That is what Aladdin did. He sold the plates to a gold merchant. He became rich and when the last plate was sold, the gold merchant asked if Aladdin had anything else to sell. He remembered the glass fruits. "They are worthless," said Aladdin, "but I will show them to you."

When the merchant saw the fruits, his eyes lit up. "Aladdin," he cried, "these are not glass fruits. They are priceless rubies, diamonds and emeralds. Each one is worth a king's ransom."

Aladdin was delighted. But he decided not to sell them. 'I will hide them until I need more money,' he thought. 'Maybe I will have a need for them one day.'

The weeks passed and Aladdin went about his new business. He spent all his time in the market learning how to be a merchant.

It happened one day that the Sultan of the city was returning from a visit to a foreign country. His young daughter, Buddir al Buddoor, was travelling with him. On pain of death no one was allowed to look upon her beauty. The Sultan's emirs, chamberlains and lords went ahead of the Sultan, warning everyone on the road to bow their heads as she passed.

As the Sultan's horses came in sight, Aladdin's mind turned to mischief. He had heard about the lovely princess and could not resist peeping at her from behind a pillar.

"O Allah, what beauty!" cried Aladdin as she passed. "She is a moon of moons and a sun of suns. There can be no one more beautiful." Aladdin fell instantly in love with her.

That night when he returned home, he was so in love he could not eat. "What's the matter?" asked his mother. "Are you ill? Shall I call a doctor?"

"Mother," said Aladdin, "I am not ill. I am in love. I shall not rest until I have married the Sultan's daughter."

"What nonsense is this," she said. "You can never marry a Sultan's daughter. You are the son of a poor tailor."

Nothing could change Aladdin's mind. "I shall marry Buddir al Buddoor," he said, "and what is more I know how I shall win her hand." Aladdin went to the secret hiding place in his bedroom. He carefully removed his collection of glass fruits, the stones he now knew to be rubies, diamonds and emeralds. He took them to his mother.

"Each day the Sultan holds court to listen to complaints and requests from his people," said Aladdin. "You must take these precious stones and

138

give them to the Sultan, offer them in exchange for the hand of his daughter in marriage."

Aladdin's mother looked at the stones. "They are worthy of a Sultan's daughter," she said, "but however rich your gift, the Sultan will soon discover you are a poor tailor's son."

"Do as I bid, mother," pleaded Aladdin. "I will never be happy otherwise."

Aladdin's mother was very frightened of going to see the Sultan. But at last she plucked up courage. The next morning she put the stones on a tray, covered them with a cloth and set off. At the palace gates her legs began to tremble. 'Surely the Sultan will throw me into the dungeon for daring to make such a request,' she thought.

The great doors of the palace opened. Aladdin's mother entered. She was led into the Sultan's court. His emirs, chamberlains and lords stared at the tray, wondering what lay beneath the cloth. The Vizier, the Sultan's chief advisor, watched closely too.

"Come forward, woman," said the Sultan. "Tell me what you have come to ask."

Aladdin's mother hardly dared speak for a moment. "My lord," she began hesitantly. "Forgive me for what I am about to ask."

"Ask what you will," said the Sultan.

"My son, Aladdin, seeks your daughter's hand in marriage," she said.

There was silence in the court for a moment. Then the Sultan began to smile. The smile turned into a laugh and the laugh became a great guffaw. "Ho! Ho! Ho! Your son would marry my daughter, would he?"

Aladdin's mother bravely continued. "My son has sent some fruits as a gift."

When the Sultan heard that Aladdin expected to win his daughter

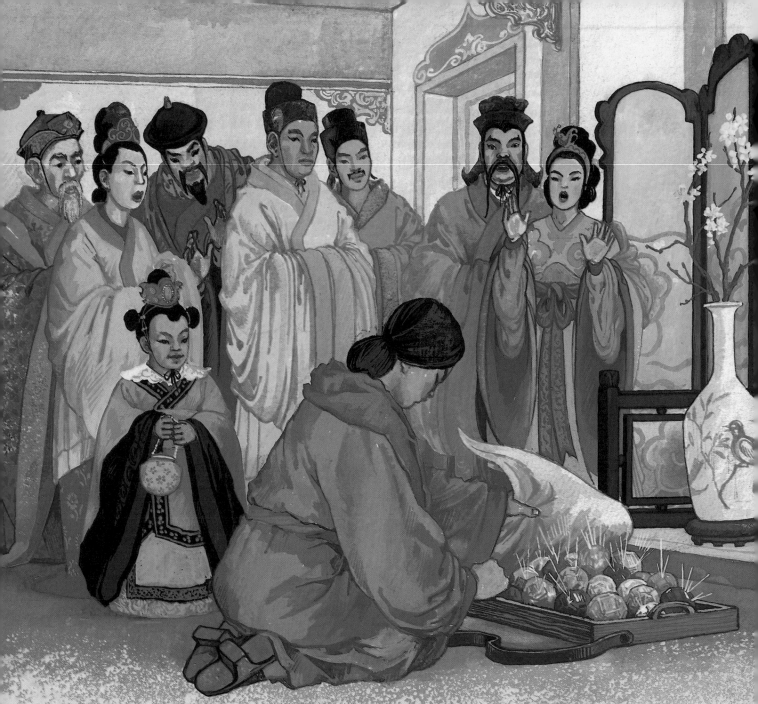

with a gift of fruits, he roared even louder. He gripped the sides of his throne to stop himself from falling off.

Just then Aladdin's mother removed the cloth from the tray. The light caught the precious stones and brought the Sultan's laughter to a sudden end. He was dazzled by their brightness, shielding his eyes from the sparkling glare.

"By Allah," said the surprised Sultan.

"Allah be praised," said the admiring emirs.

"Delicious fruits indeed," said the lords.

"Each one is worth a fortune," said the Vizier.

The Sultan could not take his eyes off the jewels. "There is nothing so precious in my treasure house," he said, beckoning to the Vizier.

"Is this not a fair prize for my daughter?"

Now, the Vizier had a son and he wanted him to marry the Princess. "O mighty Sultan," he whispered in his master's ear, "you did promise your daughter to my son."

The Sultan thought for a moment and then replied in hushed tones, "I give you three months to find something more precious than these jewels. If you cannot, then Aladdin shall marry my daughter."

"It is impossible, Master," he replied. "There is nothing more precious in Allah's kingdom."

The Sultan turned to Aladdin's mother. "Return to your son and tell him that in three months he shall marry my daughter. That is my promise."

She hurried home to tell Aladdin the news. How happy he was and as the weeks passed Aladdin prepared for the wedding. But one morning he reached the market and saw that a huge celebration was planned. All the houses were decorated and the people were in cheerful mood.

"What is the reason for this celebration?" he asked a passer-by.

"Why, you must have heard. The Sultan's daughter is to marry the Vizier's son today."

"The Sultan has forgotten his promise," Aladdin cried.

Aladdin ran home. He went straight to his bedroom and fell, weeping, on his bed. He cried himself to sleep. It was dark when he awoke. 'The Princess will have married the Vizier's son by now,' he thought, sadly. Suddenly Aladdin had an idea. He leapt from his bed and went to his secret hiding place. He took out the lamp and rubbed it.

Whoosh! The Genie appeared on his command. "O Master of the Lamp," said the Genie, "your wish is my command."

"Slave of the Lamp," cried Aladdin. "When the Vizier's son comes to Buddir al Buddoor's room on this their wedding night, I want you to play a trick on him. Now listen, this is what I want you to do."

"Aha! What mischief does Aladdin plan?" cried King Shabriar.

"If you will allow me, I shall tell you the rest of the story tomorrow night," replied Sheherezade.

"So be it," said the King. "Until tomorrow night."

The next evening Sheherezade continued her story.

3 The Sorcerer's Return

That night the Vizier's son, a foolish and boastful young man, bathed and dressed himself in his finest nightshirt. "Oh, how handsome I am," he said. "How lucky the Princess is to have married me."

He reached the Princess's room and entered. The Princess was sitting in bed. She could not believe her eyes when she saw what happened next. The Vizier's son could not understand it either. An invisible force grabbed him by the neck and marched him across the room to a large jug. His head was bent down and pushed firmly inside. The jug trapped him by his ears.

"Let me out," he shrieked, his voice echoing in the bottom of the jug. The mysterious force had not finished its mischief. It also glued the feet of the Vizier's son to the floor. He could not move one step. The Princess burst into tears. All night she called on the Vizier's son to free himself. There was nothing he could do. He just gurgled angrily into the jug, unable to move.

In the morning, as if by magic, the Vizier's son was released from his ridiculous position. But every night for a week, the same thing happened. The Princess never dared tell the Sultan what the trouble was, but she grew so unhappy that eventually he decided to end the marriage.

Aladdin laughed and danced with joy when he heard the news. The next day he went to the Sultan's palace. "O mighty Sultan, three months have passed," he said. "You promised me the hand of Princess Buddir al Buddoor."

"That is true," said the Sultan, "but we shall let her decide if she wishes to marry you. Bring in the Princess," he called.

Princess Buddir al Buddoor had never set eyes on Aladdin before. When she was brought in, her eyes lit up with happiness. "I could not hope to find a more handsome Prince," she said, smiling.

"Then you shall be married tomorrow," said the Sultan.

"That will give me plenty of time to build a palace," said Aladdin.

"A palace? You can build a palace in just one night?" asked the Sultan.

"Yes," said Aladdin. "I shall build it opposite your gates so you can come and visit your daughter whenever you want."

Aladdin ran home and took out the magic lamp. "Slave of the Lamp,"

he said, "build me a palace and place it opposite the Sultan's gates."

The next morning the Sultan arose and as the great palace gates opened he was met by the most amazing sight he had ever seen.

"A palace!" he cried. "By Allah, Aladdin has kept his promise." In front of him stood the finest palace he had ever seen. Its gate was studded with jewels and the towers were topped with gold. The Sultan summoned his daughter to see the marvellous building. The Slave of the Lamp had left nothing undone. Every room was furnished in great luxury.

Now everything was ready for the wedding. Yet a black cloud was about to threaten the happy couple's day. Unknown to them all, the wicked sorcerer, who had left Aladdin for dead in the cavern, was even now close by. When he discovered that Aladdin was alive, he had set out from his home in Africa. He reached China and the Sultan's city on the very day of the wedding.

He saw Aladdin's great palace and realised it was the work of the Slave of the Lamp. "Demons and dragons," he screeched. "Devils fly about your head, Aladdin. I shall have that lamp now."

The sorcerer had a plan. He went to the market and bought a dozen new brass lamps. Hanging them about his neck on a rope, he walked beneath

the palace walls. "New lamps for old!" he cried. "New lamps for old!"

Aladdin had just left the palace to go hunting. He didn't see the wicked sorcerer arrive. The Princess was busy inside the palace watching the servants prepare the wedding feast. She heard the lamp-seller's call.

Now, it happened that Aladdin had brought the magic lamp to the palace. He had not yet had time to hide it. The Princess saw it among his possessions. She could not understand why Aladdin wanted to keep such an old lamp.

'New lamps for old?' she thought. 'I shall give Aladdin a surprise.'

The Princess took the old lamp to the palace gates and called to the man with the new lamps. "I have an old lamp," she said. "Will you give me a new one for it?"

The sorcerer's eyes gleamed with delight. "Let me see it," he said. The Princess handed over the lamp. As soon as his greedy hands had grasped it, the sorcerer let out a hideous cry and ran off. The new lamps fell from his neck and clattered onto the road. The sorcerer was gone in a cloud of dust.

The sorcerer didn't stop running until he was out of the city. He stopped by the side of the road and held the lamp in his hands. With a look of triumph on his face, he began to rub it.

Whoosh! The Genie appeared. "Master of the Lamp, your wish is my command."

"Slave of the Lamp," said the sorcerer, "obey my wish. Take Aladdin's palace and his Princess to my country in Africa and transport me there too."

"Your wish is my command," said the Genie, quickly disappearing once more.

In the city the streets were crowded with people arriving for the

wedding. Thousands stood outside the palace waiting for Aladdin to arrive. Suddenly a swirling black cloud swept towards the palace. Amid cries of terror, it hid all in its path. Darkness covered the city. It was some time before the cloud lifted and the people could see again.

"Look!" cried the crowd. "The palace has gone." Indeed not a stone stood where the palace had been. "There!" shouted the crowd, pointing to the sky. "The cloud has carried the palace away." In the distance the black cloud was racing towards the horizon. On top of it stood the palace in all its glory.

When the Sultan saw what had happened he flew into a rage. "My daughter! My daughter! Who has stolen my daughter?"

He was so angry he sent his men to arrest Aladdin and bring him back in chains. "Bring my executioner," he cried. "I shall have Aladdin's head for this treachery."

Aladdin was brought before the Sultan. "Cut off his head!" he ordered.

"Great Sultan," cried Aladdin, "give me a day and I will return your daughter to you . . . my palace too."

The Sultan liked Aladdin and decided to give him a last chance. "Go, Aladdin. I will give you a day. If you have not found my daughter by nightfall, you will answer with your head."

Aladdin hurried out of the Sultan's palace and ran through the city until he was out in the country alone. "Now," he murmured, rubbing the ring on his finger, "I shall find that evil sorcerer. He has surely returned and stolen my Princess."

Whoosh! The Slave of the Ring appeared. "Master of the Ring, your wish is my command," the Genie boomed.

"Quick," said Aladdin. "Tell me what has happened to my Princess."

151

The Genie explained all that had happened. "Bring the palace, the Princess and the lamp here this minute," he ordered.

The Genie's reply was unexpected. "I cannot," he said. "I have no power to change an order given by the Master of the Lamp."

Aladdin's hopes fell. But then he thought again. "Slave of the Ring, if you cannot bring me what I want, take me to the Princess and the palace."

"Your wish is my command, o Master."

The next thing Aladdin knew he was in Africa, standing beneath a window of his palace. He could hear the sound of sobbing coming from inside. "It is my Princess," he cried.

He called out and soon she appeared at the window. "My beloved Aladdin," she wept. "I knew you would come to rescue me."

"Quick! Where is the sorcerer? Where is the lamp you gave him?"

The Princess said the sorcerer was away from the castle. "He always carries the lamp with him," she said. "He will be back soon."

Aladdin quickly made his plan. He called on the Genie of the Ring to help once more. "Bring me a sleeping potion," he ordered. Later, when all was arranged, Aladdin hid behind a curtain in the Princess's room and waited. Soon the sorcerer returned home. The lamp was hanging from his neck.

The sorcerer was surprised to see that the Princess was not crying. "Are you happier in your new home?" he asked.

He was delighted to hear the Princess's answer. "Yes," she said, "but it is so hot. Come, let us have a cooling drink." The Princess gave the sorcerer a large silver cup. He was so thirsty he drank it all in one gulp. The potion quickly did its work. First the sorcerer let out a small yawn, then a bigger one and finally a gigantic yawn.

"What's the matter with me," he said, rubbing his eyes. "I feel so slee . . ."

The sorcerer fell down on a cushion. Even as his eyes began to close he saw Aladdin appear from his hiding place. It was too late. The sorcerer could do nothing. His eyelids grew heavier and heavier and finally closed over his evil eyes. Only the Slave of the Ring knew how strong the potion was. The sorcerer would sleep for fifty years.

Aladdin rushed over to the sorcerer and took the lamp from his neck, "Now I am Master of the Lamp again," he cried. "Come, we must hurry home. Have you forgotten?"

"Forgotten?" said the Princess.

"It is still our wedding day," said Aladdin. "Today is the day the poor tailor's son marries the Sultan's daughter. We must fly." He rubbed the lamp and the Genie appeared. "Take us back to China," ordered Aladdin, "and let the palace travel with us."

The Sultan was walking sadly in his courtyard when he saw a dark cloud appear on the horizon. "What's this?" he said, staring at something on top of the cloud. "Why, it's Aladdin's palace!" he shouted.

Soon the city was hidden by the cloud. When it cleared, before the Sultan's eyes stood Aladdin's palace. Looking out from a window were Aladdin and the Princess.

There was a happy reunion. The Sultan hugged his daughter and forgave Aladdin. "By Allah, I would have had your head if you had not brought my daughter back," he laughed. "But enough of that. Your wedding awaits."

Aladdin and Princess Buddir al Buddoor were married that day.

It was a happy celebration with much feasting and drinking. The streets were full of joyful people, who, like the Sultan, had grown to love Aladdin.

Aladdin and the Princess lived happily in their grand palace for many years. When the Sultan died, Aladdin took his place on the throne.

And that is the story of how the poor tailor's son married a beautiful Princess and became a Sultan.

King Shabriar smiled in delight. "Aladdin was right," said the King. "He vowed he would marry the Princess and he said their story would be told for evermore."

"They will tell it long after we have gone," answered Sheherezade.

The story of Aladdin was not the last tale the Princess told the King. She continued to entertain him with great adventures, romances and mysteries for a thousand and one nights.

King Shabriar grew to love his story-telling Princess. "O Princess," he said one day. "How could I ever slay one as beautiful as you? Besides, who will tell me stories if you are not by my side? You must never leave me."

The Princess never did leave the King. They spent the rest of their lives happily together, and both lived to be a hundred years old. Yet when they died, their tale was never forgotten. It is still told today.

It is called the story of the Arabian Nights.